# BENEATH US THE STARS

# BENEATH US THE STARS

## DAVID WILTSHIRE

THORNDIKE
CHIVERS

This Large Print edition is published by Thorndike Press, Waterville, Maine, USA and by BBC Audiobooks Ltd, Bath, England.

Thorndike Press is an imprint of Thomson Gale, a part of The Thomson Corporation.

Thorndike is a trademark and used herein under license.

The text of this Large Print edition is unabridged.

Other aspects of the book may vary from the original edition.

Set in 16 pt. Plantin.

**LIBRARY OF CONGRESS CATALOGING-IN-PUBLICATION DATA**

Wiltshire, David, 1935–
    Beneath us the stars / by David Wiltshire. — Large print ed.
        p. cm. — (Thorndike press large print clean read)
    ISBN-13: 978-0-7862-9685-9 (alk. paper)
    ISBN-10: 0-7862-9685-2 (alk. paper)
        1. Women college teachers — Great Britain — Fiction. 2. Air pilots,
    Military — Great Britain — Fiction. 3. Americans — Great Britain —
    Fiction. 4. World War, 1939–1945 — Missing in action — Fiction. 5. Large
    type books. I. Title.
    PR6073.I47535B46  2007
    823'.914—dc22                                                      2007014350

BRITISH LIBRARY CATALOGUING-IN-PUBLICATION DATA AVAILABLE

Published in 2007 in the U.S. by arrangement with Robert Hale Limited.
Published in 2007 in the U.K. by arrangement with the author.

U.K. Hardcover: 978 1 405 64144 9 (Chivers Large Print)
U.K. Softcover: 978 1 405 64145 6 (Camden Large Print)

Printed in the United States of America on permanent paper
10 9 8 7 6 5 4 3 2 1

THE LAST ENEMY THAT SHALL BE
DESTROYED IS DEATH

St Paul's First Epistle to the Corinthians
XV, 26

*For Peggy Wiltshire*

# AUTHOR'S NOTE

My thanks to June Elks for deciphering my handwriting with her usual good humour, and to Brian Howard for evolving the title over a bottle of wine.

David Wiltshire

# PROLOGUE

The roar of the piston engine filled the small cabin as the plane flew straight and level, almost as fast as a fighter of an earlier age.

Far below, where columns of sunlight uninterrupted by the towering clouds touched its surface, the water sparkled like puddles of molten silver in a sea of lead.

Caught in the clear light, the glinting disc of the unseen propeller plunged into cloud, dulled, then flashed anew as it emerged into an abyss between the sun-kissed mountains of the sky.

Abruptly the engine throttled back, the roar in the cabin replaced by the shrieking slipstream — and the sound of Glenn Miller's *Moonlight Serenade.*

As the saxophones continued the haunting melody, the wind slowly subsided, became only a whisper. The propeller now clearly seen, flicked erratically as the plane lost flying speed, became unstable, then finally ceased to fly. The nose dropped, pointed towards the surface 10,000 feet below, began to fall.

Suddenly the motor picked up, the roar rising and rising until the tortured, over-loaded engine reached the pitch of a dive-bomber.

Banking away to the right the plane dwindled to a speck, eventually could no longer be distinguished, disappearing into the ever changing silver and slate-blue shadows on the surface of the cold water.

The North Sea.

The final resting place of so many.

# CHAPTER ONE

He had lain awake for over an hour, the pain in his side leaving him in a cold sweat. He'd tried not to wake his wife but he'd eventually felt her stir.

'Bill — are you awake?'

'It's OK, Mary — just going to the bathroom.'

Light flooded the room as she turned on her bedside lamp. 'Is it the pain?'

He knew it was no good pretending, not with Mary.

'Just a little.'

Bill hauled himself up on to his elbows. At eighty-five his once dark hair was now white and thinning, the intense blue eyes that had so captivated her in their twenties, paler, but still carrying in them something of the far distant look of the hunter in the sky he used to be. In those wild dangerous days of his youth the ability to see the tiniest of specks was often the difference between life and death.

He pulled back the rumpled cover and swung his legs to the floor.

'You go back to sleep, sweetie — put the light out.' There was still, after all the years in England, an American inflection in his drawl.

As he shuffled, angular frame bent and stiff, to the *en suite,* Mary reached for the switch. 'Don't stub your toe.' In the dark when he returned, he climbed in and cuddled up to her, unaware of the tears in her eyes.

She had lived all her adult life frightened of mortality. Oh, she had strong views on the spiritual existence of mankind, but the awful truth was that here and now, the life of the man she loved was impermanent, fragile, that it could cease to exist without warning. When she'd first met him in those dark days of war, that could have happened any day, day in day out. But now, with the advancement of years she knew that their time was inevitably running out. Loving anyone left you vulnerable.

Next morning Bill picked two more slices of toast from the machine, added them to a pile on a plate, and took it over to the window table of the apartment.

The morning rush hour in the road outside was well under way.

'There you go.' He set the plate down as Mary swung her wheelchair up to the table. Her long white hair crowned a face that despite the ravages of time, still hinted at the beauty that had taken his breath away so many years ago.

They sat in silence, busying themselves with butter and marmalade and sipping coffee. Bill took two quick bites of his toast, then folded his paper back on itself and then again before setting it beside his plate. Occasionally he laid down the slice of toast, sipped his coffee, and resumed eating, all without taking his eyes from the newsprint.

Mary had her paper too, but this morning she kept surreptitiously glancing at him.

At last she spoke. 'Traffic looks heavy. Maybe we'd better go earlier.'

He glanced up. 'Nice day, what say we walk?'

She frowned, 'You'll be too tired to push me all the way home.'

Snorting, he took the marmalade-pot and fished in it with his knife.

'Nonsense. The doc's not going to do anything today. Just give me the results, probably tell me another pleasure in life must be denied.'

Not believing him for one moment, she

15

nevertheless nodded. 'All right, but only if you promise we'll have a taxi back if you're tired.'

Bill raised his hand in a mock copy of someone taking an oath.

'I promise so to do.'

He returned to his paper. He did not see the look of love and worry on her face. But he didn't need to. After sixty years the two of them seemed to know each others' mind as if it were their own.

They started out early, Bill pushing Mary in her chair, stopping in a lane to pick a few blackberries. He gave her half. She laughed at the staining on his tongue. 'Mr Parsons is going to have a fit when he sees that.'

At last they reached an entrance, passing a sign reading *Welcome to Addenbrooke's Hospital, Cambridge.*

The waiting-area for the outpatients was packed. Several women manned a large reception desk, shifting through buff-coloured files and answering phones. Bill parked Mary at the end of a row of chairs and, after checking in, sat alongside her, doing *The Times* crossword. It was Mary who did most of the solving. He was just triumphantly getting one for a change when they became conscious of a nurse standing over them.

'Mr Anderson?'

Bill nodded.

'Would you like to come through?'

He looked at Mary. 'Here we go.'

She squeezed his forearm. 'Good luck.'

She watched her husband follow the nurse, quite swiftly considering the limp from his war wound, and only a little bowed after all these years.

Quickly she returned to the crossword, changed what he had just proposed, tried to carry on as normal in spite of her desperate worry. After all her years at Bletchley Park, although not one of the cryptographers — she was in the department that analysed the different use of language regionally in Germany and Italy — she found the crossword very easy. She had completed it by the time Bill had finished redressing and was facing Mr Parsons, a tall man in a white coat that was not quite big enough for him, stethoscope dangling from his neck. The surgeon completed his notes, carefully replacing the cap on his fountain pen.

'Please do sit down, Mr Anderson.'

Bill took the offered seat.

There was a moment's silence as Parsons studied the pen, held between his two hands, obviously trying to find the right words.

Bill's eyes narrowed. 'Give it to me straight — please.'

The surgeon looked up. There was no avoiding the command — even though it had been spoken politely, quietly. Maybe it was the accent.

'You have a tumour in the colon.'

The face before him didn't seem to register any emotion. He knew from his notes somewhere that the man had had a distinguished war. Perhaps he'd grown accustomed to the idea of death. His own line of thought was interrupted by his patient.

'Is it benign or malignant?'

Parsons chose his words carefully. 'It is a malignant form, but with surgical intervention and some therapy your expectations for a further — say, five years, would not be unthinkable.'

At last the face changed, into an ironic smile.

'For a man of my age another five years is a mixed blessing indeed.'

The consultant smiled back weakly, not sure how to take the remark.

'You will have to have a colostomy of course. You do understand what I mean, Mr Anderson?'

Bill shook his head slowly and emphatically. 'No.'

Mr Parsons mistook what he meant, and pulled a sheet of paper towards him, intent on sketching out in diagrammatic form what had to be done. 'Well, we have to make a new opening for the gut, and a bag is —'

Bill stopped him.

'I mean no — I won't proceed.'

Perplexed, the surgeon scratched the corner of his forehead. 'I know it sounds awful, but it's really something you can, with a little adaptation to your way of life —'

Bill half-raised a hand.

'Look Mr Parsons, I appreciate you are trying to do your best for me, and I thank you for that. I have great confidence and respect for your ability — that has nothing to do with it.' He grunted. 'Or fear of the knife — after all I've had quite a few run-ins with surgeons in the past — they've fixed me up pretty good every time.'

The medical man's concern was evident.

'So — why not now?'

Bill sat for some time before answering.

'My wife relies on me completely — for *everything*.'

Looking relieved, the consultant said: 'My dear Mr Anderson, we can arrange through her GP and Social Services to have all the necessary cover for her while you recuperate — and beyond.'

Both knew he meant permanently.

Bill smiled weakly, really liking the man. He obviously genuinely cared for his patients.

'I know, I know. It's — well — personal. On bad days I lift her out of bed, on the loo and so on — we're an old married couple — been together a long time. It would be . . .' He gestured hopelessly.

Mr Parsons tried a last, direct approach.

'You do realize that if we do not cut it out you will succumb to the cancer?'

Bill sniffed.

'I think you mean *die* do you not, doctor?'

His lips in a tight line, Mr Parsons nodded firmly. 'I do.'

His patient considered the answer for a moment.

'How long have I got?'

Mary sat before a baby grand in their main room, furnished from a lifetime of collecting in shops and auction rooms. The standard lamps in the corners were from the fifties, small Victorian chairs were placed against the walls, while grouped in front of the fireplace were traditional sofas imported from the States in the eighties. On side tables were many silver-framed photographs, one of the very young Bill and Mary standing outside a Register Office, she in a suit with a hat and a fox-fur draped around her shoulders, he in his United States Army Air Force uniform with wings.

Others were of their children at various ages, the two girls and a boy, ending with each one of them on their graduation days. There were photographs of groups of people, celebrating past Christmases and New Years in a home very much larger than the apartment they were now occupying.

Her slim hands, showing liver spots where once there was only smooth white skin, picked out the notes of *Für Elise* as noises came from the kitchen.

Her husband's voice eventually floated out from the doorway.

'Come and get it — lunch is served.'

She stopped playing, gently lowered the lid and propelled herself into the dining-kitchen, taking her place at the table. Bill set down a dish of steaming new potatoes. Cold meats and a salad were already on the table.

He poured white wine into her glass, then his own and sat down. Mary sipped hers and looked at him over the rim of her glass.

'Surely he must have given you another appointment?'

Bill busied himself dishing out the potatoes.

'No — just said the doc would get his letter and take it from there.'

Mary remained unconvinced, accusing him. 'You're not telling me the truth.'

'Sure I am. They were his last words.' He wasn't lying, he told himself. They *had* been Mr Parsons's last words. What he hadn't told her was the rest of it.

They ate in silence for a while, only exchanging the odd word. The radio, playing Classic FM in the background, helped to fill the gaps.

At last Mary placed her knife and fork together, even though she obviously hadn't finished.

'I can't eat any more. Do you mind if I lie down for a while, I feel a little tired?'

Bill got up, suddenly concerned.

'Everything all right?'

Mary pulled back from the table.

'No — it's not, and you know it.'

She wheeled away down a short corridor, leaving him to pick up her plate glumly and put its contents into the bin before following her.

She had stopped by their bed.

Mary placed her hands around his neck as he stooped. Puffing, he straightened up and settled her on to the covers, falling forward on to her with the effort. He stood up, spent some time getting his breath back.

From her pillow she regarded him steadily. When she spoke it was very softly.

'I love you.'

He smiled down at her.

'I know. And I love you.'

Mary gazed up at him.

'Let's see, how long have we been together now? From the very beginning?'

Bill looked at his watch.

'Oh, I'd say sixty-something years, eleven hours, twenty minutes and ten — no, fourteen seconds.'

Mary nodded solemnly.

'That's about it, so don't try and hide anything from me, mister.'

Bill winced. 'I'm not —'

Mary cut him off with a wave of her hand. 'Hogwash!'

The Americanism coming from her very English voice was effective. He floundered, but before he could say anything further she closed her eyes and said: 'When I wake up we're going to take a ride.'

He frowned. 'Are we? Where?'

'To the airfield.'

Bill blinked.

'What airfield?'

She kept her eyes shut.

'You know very well where I mean. And when we get there you are going to tell me exactly — *completely* — everything he said to you this morning — right, Lieutenant?'

He gazed down at her, realized the game was up. Ruefully he murmured: 'Right, ma'am.'

He bent down. Their lips brushed.

When he pulled back she said, still with her eyes closed: 'Now bugger off!'

Grinning, he closed the door gently behind him, leant back against it, his face dissolving into immeasurable sadness. He moved into the sitting-room, his hands shaking slightly as he poured a Jack Daniel's and slumped into a chair. He took a gulp, and reached out to a wood-framed black-and-white photograph. It was Mary, aged twenty-one, hair brushed across one eye to curl down at the corner of her mouth.

Although he had been as light-hearted as he could manage for her, the surgeon's prognosis, spoken aloud, had been, despite his premonition of the seriousness of the illness, a cruel shock.

He took a sip of the whiskey, felt its warmth steadying his nerves.

Even before the morning he had been well aware of the corruptibility of the flesh —

who wasn't at his age? He already took six tablets every morning for blood pressure and cholesterol, and a further three during the day for his late-onset diabetes.

But with Parsons there had been no escape, no 'if you do this you will live for ever promise,' only the blunt, bleak truth.

The train of his life was about to run into the buffers.

He was not overtly religious, though they did go to church at Easter and Christmas. For him, the experience was more the shared spiritual atmosphere in the wonderful old college chapel that had seen so many generations go before, than any burning belief.

But he knew Mary felt differently, had very strongly held convictions — even though she was not a regular churchgoer either.

She had first blurted out her feelings one night back in 1944. Young they might have been, but life had been lived on the edge then, with death a constant companion.

He managed a weak smile at the memory of that night, so clearly recalled, as if it were yesterday — he grunted at the irony — *better* than yesterday.

Like most young men of his generation he had had to go to war. With the invincibility of youth wrapped around him, at least to begin with, he had not thought much about death; that was something that happened to someone else.

It wasn't so later.

But he'd never forgotten Mary's sudden revelation in the heightened atmosphere of that evening, even though they had never spoken of it again.

Now his life was coming to an end.

Oblivion?

Or was she going to be proved right?

He replaced the photograph, took another sip of the whiskey, tried to steady his nerves.

A hard lump had come from nowhere and made it difficult to swallow.

Bill drove the open-top MGB that he'd lovingly looked after for the last thirty years. Mary was always grumbling that since her confinement to the chair some two years ago, due to arthritis in her spine, the car was totally impractical. But secretly he guessed she was as in love with it as he was. It harked back to an age when their world was younger and freer.

Glenn Miller's orchestra was coming from the radio-cassette-player.

He pulled up at a T junction.

Mary picked up the map on her lap.

'It's left.'

He shook his head.

'Right.'

She tapped her finger on the map. 'I tell you it's left. It is twenty-five years ago since we last came. Those trees have grown since then, that's what's misleading you.'

Bill banged the steering wheel.

'I know this place like the back of my hand. For God's sake, it's etched into my memory, woman.'

Mary was unmoved.

'You daft old coot, it's left, I tell you.'

Still grumbling, he did as he was told.

'Bloody English lanes. For Christ's sake they all look the same.'

They eventually drove into a wood, later emerging into a modern commercial trading-estate.

Bill drew to a halt and surveyed the scene.

'Oh, my God.'

They sat in silence with the motor the only sound, the cassette turned off.

At last Mary said: 'Nothing's the same any more. The whole country will be built over soon.'

He put the MG into gear.

'Let's try the other side of the wood, there's a track over there.'

It was unmade, with deep depressions and

ruts. The car lurched and bounced and creaked. She didn't say anything, but the pain in her back was awful.

Eventually they were confronted by a dense hedge.

Mary pointed. 'There's a way to the left.'

'Got it.'

He spun the steering wheel. They both saw it at the same time — the remains of an old runway with lank weeds pushing up through cracks in the concrete, and with old tyre-streaks still visible. Beyond, some 400 yards away across a ploughed field there was the remains of a derelict brick building, the windows and roof long since gone, the metal work rusty and twisted.

Bill eased the car to a halt.

'That's the control tower.'

They both stood in silence, lost in the dreams of the past: — dangerous times, austere times — but a time when they were young and full of life.

# CHAPTER TWO:
## NINETEEN FORTY-FOUR

Bill pulled the cockpit hood back. Immediately the noise crowded in and smoke swirled around, coming from burning huts. Men were running everywhere, fire-bells sounded, ambulances roared past, planes were still landing; mayhem was reigning. Hands helped him unbuckle his harness and he climbed out on to the wing, then jumped to the ground, his legs almost failing him. He'd been sitting cramped up for hours. His eyes fell on a long row of tarpaulin-covered bodies.

Shuddering, Bill shouldered his parachute and pulled off his flying-helmet. His face was wringing with sweat and oil-stains. As he stumbled along his crew chief fell into step beside him.

'How was it, sir?'

Bill growled. 'The Battling Bastards of Brunswick were out in force today.' He looked wildly around. 'What the hell happened here?'

'You wouldn't believe it, sir, but half an hour ago a lone Heinkel dropped a stick of bombs right on top of the mess hall and the cookhouse — blew them to smithereens.'

Another ambulance went past and the smoke seemed to thicken.

Coughing, Bill asked: 'Casualties?'

The crew chief cleared his throat and spat on the ground. 'Yes, sir, twenty-three dead, as many wounded. He sneaked up on us right down on the deck. Sun was blinding. Gone before we knew it. Hardly a gun fired. Classic nuisance raid.'

Bill scowled. 'Nuisance? Tell that to them.' He jerked his hand at the tarp-covered figures. 'Did the RAF get him?'

'Couldn't tell you, sir.'

Bill reacted savagely. 'God damn it. Who the hell is supposed to be defending this place when we're away?'

With his legs stronger he left his crew chief behind and strode rapidly towards a hut with a large G painted on its side, and entered.

Inside were rows of tables with intelligence officers taking notes from aircrew.

Bill slumped down in an empty chair and held up a chipped enamel cup, into which an airman poured black coffee. The intelligence officer sitting before him added a generous slug of whisky.

He muttered his thanks.

The man let him take a few sips before he asked: 'Bad one?'

Bill, his anger gone and the exhaustion hitting him like a freight train, seemed almost physically to shrink. 'No more than usual.'

The intelligence officer dropped his gaze to the cup. It was shaking.

The walls of the Officers Club were decorated with bits of German aircraft and pin-ups. Dance-music sounded in the background. Bill sat at the bar, staring morosely into his glass of beer, smoke curling up from the neglected cigarette held in his hand. A mature-looking major slid quietly on to the stool beside him, and indicated without speaking to the barman that he too would have a beer like Bill's.

Nobody said anything until the major had had his first couple of sips.

Speaking to the rows of bottles on display before him he said: 'I'm ordering a one-week pass for you — with immediate effect.'

Bill looked up, noticed the doctor for the first time.

'Doc, I can't. We need every ship we can

31

get into the air. It's impossible. Anyway, why are you picking on me?'

The flight-surgeon chopped his hand decisively down to emphasize the point.

'Ordering, Bill — *ordering.* It's cut already. Go down to London, go anywhere, have some fun. For God's sake, man, you've been in the firing-line non-stop ever since you got here.'

Bill shook his head.

'There are others who need it more than me.'

The doctor sighed. 'OK, I knew it wasn't going to be easy, so I've revoked your fitness to fly — to be reviewed in one week.'

Before Bill could say anything he added: 'Go first thing in the morning — hell, you'll be back soon enough and I guess there will still be plenty of war for everyone.'

Later that night he lay on his bunk, smoking a Lucky Strike, staring up at the ceiling, listening to the faraway rumble of hundreds of heavy bombers heading out to sea. The Royal Air Force. Round the clock.

He couldn't sleep — not without the doc's pills, and since he wasn't going on the job in the morning he'd decided not to pop one.

His mind was racing. What would he do for the week? London? The Washington

Club or 100 Piccadilly, or maybe even the Woolly Lamb, Chappies or Eve's? The thought of mooching around with all the thousands of GIs flooding the bars, the streets and the theatres wasn't attractive. The whole area was jokingly called the American Colony. Then there were all the loose women hanging around the doorways, the so-called Piccadilly Commandos; he shuddered, no, definitely not London. He would have liked to go to a country hotel, get away from it all to somewhere peaceful, but he didn't know any, and in any case, they were difficult to get at. That left Cambridge or Norwich.

He decided on Cambridge — and a look around the colleges.

It was a decision that was to alter his life.

On a cold winter's day he watched the countryside go slowly past the carriage window, the steam and smoke from the engine drifting away across the meadows to merge with the fog still hanging around. Dripping trees loomed ghostlike from the murk.

There had been no squadron take-off that morning, all wing operations cancelled because of the weather. The irony of it did not escape him.

The train stopped several times for no apparent reason, though he'd been told by a local that they often did, due to poor coal.

The compartment was freezing, there was no heating. Muffled voices, coughing, and occasional shouts and laughter carried in the silence. Troops with kitbags used as seats blocked the corridor which was blue with acrid cigarette smoke.

By the time they steamed into Cambridge he'd had enough. He chose to walk into town rather than wait for one of the shared taxis, many with bags of gas on their roofs, which was used as fuel.

When he started to pass Georgian buildings, then later great high walls and sixteenth-century architecture, his spirits lifted. True, he'd flown over the place a couple of times, but it was here on the streets that you really got the flavour of the ancient town and its university.

He'd managed to find a small hotel through the American Red Cross Club, who'd booked it for him. Like all the public places in England it had a war-weary look about it: of times, now gone, when the carpets, the curtains, the wallpaper had obviously been bright and new. Now it was all faded and threadbare, and needed a good clean.

Still, a cheerful fire of logs burned in the grate of the small lounge, with its aspidistras and brass ornaments.

After checking in he had a quick drink of warm and watery beer at the bar, where he was served by a man in his late sixties with a shiny bald head, who doubled as the porter. When Bill told him he was hoping to see some of the sights he found an old booklet and pushed at Bill over the counter.

'There's all the colleges in there, and it shows you how to get down to the Backs by the river. Course, nothing like it was pre-war, sir, but the buildings are much the same, 'cept for some of the windows being protected.'

Bill emerged into a raw but now sunny early afternoon, consulted the pull-out map, and struck out for the first of his targets.

He found it and paused before a stone archway, admiring the shield and coat of arms above, and the figures carved in stone.

He took a tentative step or two into the stone passageway, from where there was a view of manicured grass beyond. A windowed kiosk was set in one wall.

'Can I help you, sir?'

Bill stopped. A man in a porter's uniform was addressing him through a pulled-back window.

He crossed to him.

'Ah, yeah. I was hoping to see over the college.' He tapped the guide. 'Particularly the chapel and the library.'

The man leaned further out and pointed. 'Chapel's in use at the moment but the library is free. Cross to that corner — but don't go on the grass, that's for Fellows only. Through the passage and you'll see the entrance on your right.'

Bill grinned. 'Many thanks.'

He ambled out into the quad, stood for a moment admiring the ivy-clad Tudor buildings with their great clusters of spiralled chimneys, then slowly made his way to the far corner. He looked back. The porter was still watching him. He gave an exaggerated salute, and received a friendly wave.

The library was breathtaking. He gazed around at the lovely wooden ceiling, at the ancient leather-bound and gold-tooled books that lined the walls, and the long oak tables and benches. He examined some of the student initials and dates carved all over the surface. One said J.B, 1776. Some scholar had whiled away his time, left his mark, as across the ocean England was losing a colony: his country was being born. He trailed his finger over the carved signature, before moving on. At the far end were two large windows. Bill swung his leg over the rope that hung between two moveable wooden posts and studied the stained-glass frieze that ran along their margins. Beyond, through the clear but obviously hand-made panes he could see another smaller court-yard with seats and a lime-tree.

A female voice suddenly cut into his reverie.

'What are you doing here?'

He turned. Standing there was a young, fresh-faced woman who had just come through a small arched side door, a couple of books were clasped to her chest. Stunned, Bill didn't reply for a moment. She had a beautiful clear complexion, her skin was unblemished, pink and healthy, washed by the rains of England, never burnt by a raging sun. It was topped with wavy dark hair cut to such a length that it ended tantalizingly near the corner of her mouth, which, though devoid of lipstick, was pink and firm. But it was her eyes really that made such an impression on him. Clear, intelligent, full of . . . he couldn't think what. Life? Innocence? But they were challenging at the moment.

'Well? Didn't you see the notice? This section is not open to the public.' Her tone was sharp, her English accent like cut glass.

At last Bill found his voice. 'I'm sorry, I guess I'm just too inquisitive for my own good, but this is such a beautiful old building, I couldn't resist seeing it all.'

Mary reddened — knew she was doing so and was embarrassed and angry by the realization. 'Well, you shouldn't be here really,' she snapped, instantly regretting her tone. My God, she thought, I am behaving like a fourteen-year-old prefect. Well, not *herself* at fourteen, for she'd been remarkably backward at that age. But coming through the door, thinking about an interpretation of a low German dialect, she had been confronted by a man in uniform. When the officer had turned round, he was as handsome as any hero had been in her innocent adolescent dreams of a few years ago, with dark hair and blue eyes, lean and muscular.

But what had made her so breathless, so shaken, was his undisguised interest in her.

As usual, she had hidden her shyness by being aggressive.

He nodded at her books. 'Sorry, I'll leave you to it.'

To her astonishment she set the books down, instinctively pulled her cardigan protectively around her, and said: 'There is no need.' She waved a hand at a bookcase in the corner by the door she had just come through. 'There are some first editions of note in there. I can unlock it and show you them — if you're interested, that is?'

Bill grinned, and with that grin the warmth just flowed through her.

'I would like that very much.'

She walked to the cabinet on legs that seemed somehow to have lost their strength. Conscious of his eyes on her back she had difficulty with the lock — her hands seemed inordinately clumsy.

She looked up — saw his reflection. Their eyes met. At that moment the lock clicked and she drew the door open, half-turning to indicate one of the shelves.

'There we are. There are some American ones there — you are American, aren't you?'

He grinned mischievously and came closer.

'You guessed right — pretty obvious, uh?'

She flapped a hand which then fluttered nervously at her throat.

'The uniform — and the voice. . . .'

'Ah, the accent.'

He stood beside her, scanning the shelves. He was tall, and his uniform with its dark tunic and pale creamy-pink close-fitting trousers, fitted his lean figure like a glove — so different from the British lads in their coarse cloth and ill-fitting battledress blouses.

His hand paused over a book.

'May I?'

She nodded. 'Of course.'

He took one down, slowly turned the pages, and murmured appreciatively.

'I'll be damned, Samuel Taylor Coleridge.'

He flipped the pages, then read aloud in a rich melodious voice that made her spine tingle.

'In Xanadu did Kubla Khan
A stately pleasure-dome decree:
Where Alph, the sacred river ran
Through caverns measureless to man
Down to a sunless sea.'

He stopped abruptly, feeling a shiver run down his own spine.

The North Sea was always sunless.

He looked up, closed the book and held it out to her.

'Like being back at school.'

She replaced it on the shelf and closed the cabinet. When she turned there was an air of expectancy.

Bill cleared his throat nervously.

'How very rude of me — I haven't introduced myself.' He held out his hand. 'I'm

Lieutenant Bill Anderson.'

She took the hand. It was firm, even bony. 'Doctor Rice.'

Her eyes were just about level with the small wings on his breast.

'You are in the Air Force?'

Bill shrugged. 'Yes, I guess it shows. And you, what branch of medicine are you in?'

Flustered she waved a hand around. 'No — no. I'm a doctor of philosophy with the temporary wartime status of a research fellow. My degrees are from London.'

He pulled a face.

'You don't much look like a fellow to me — far too pretty.'

She blushed wildly, to his pleasure and her irritation.

'It's a sort of university position. I research in languages, mostly dead ones.'

'Ah, I see.'

Swiftly she added, feeling that it seemed inadequate; 'I do do some work for the War Office though. We've all got to do everything we can during these dreadful times.'

He nodded. 'What sort of work would that be — translating?'

Her bright beautiful face creased into horror.

'Good heavens, I can't tell you that.' Even her parents knew nothing of the evaluation of transcripts she did at Bletchley Park.

Quickly Bill raised both hands. 'Of course, silly of me to ask. I should know better. I'm sorry.'

In the silence they were both aware of a moment of awkwardness and indecision.

'Say, can I buy you a coffee or something?'

His words were matched at the same time by hers as she blurted out: 'Would you like to have some tea?'

After a second, the realization that they had both been labouring with the same idea made them relax somewhat. She checked her watch.

'We can go to the upper common room.'

Bill nodded at her books on the table. 'What about your work? I don't want to interfere.'

But she was already moving off.

'Oh that can wait. Half an hour won't matter.'

He obediently followed her, leaping ahead to open doors. She smiled her thanks.

'I must apologize, I'm not usually this forward. It's the war — I blame everything on the war.'

He chuckled.

'Me too. Despite what you may have heard about us Yanks, this is not like me at all.'

In an oak-panelled room they stood in line

and drew coffee from a large battered urn.

She led the way as they took their cups to a table and sat down. 'It used to be served properly, but all the younger men are away.'

When he sipped the warm liquid Bill couldn't help giving an involuntary wince, for which she found herself apologizing — maddingly — yet again.

'Sorry, I suppose you get the real thing.'

Bill made a mental note to be more careful in the future. Their hosts had been at total war in the Atlantic now for four years. They had rationing and shortages of everything.

'Yes — it's not so bad for us. You folks have to put up with a lot.'

Feeling uncomfortable he changed the subject.

'How old did you say this college is?'

She propped her elbows on the table and raised the cup to her lips with two hands. She looked at him over the brim. 'Founded fifteen ninety-one. This part built — sixteen-ten and something or other.'

In disbelief Bill shook his head.

'That's amazing. Do you know, this is the oldest building I've ever been in. It's wonderful.'

She snorted.

'You ought to be here when there is a fen

blow — it's freezing. I need to wear the boots my mother gave me, all the time — even in bed.'

He chuckled.

'You should try our airfield.'

She eventually plucked up courage to ask about him.

'Have you been here long?'

'Eight months. This is my first furlough.'

'And you are staying in Cambridge?'

Nodding, he beamed. 'Yes, I was lucky. My hotel is right here in town.'

She looked away. 'I thought you people normally went up to London.'

He raised an eyebrow. 'You people?'

She shifted uncomfortably.

'Sorry — I meant — well, you know — you airforce types . . .' She tailed off lamely.

Bill, who couldn't take his eyes off her, felt a moment of panic. 'We've got a bad reputation, huh?'

One delightful eyebrow rose as she teased: 'No — no; exuberant perhaps.'

He shook his head. 'Well, sometimes the boys need to let off a little steam. London? Not for me. Frankly I just couldn't face it. I'm not a big-city fan at the best of times, so Cambridge seemed like a good idea. I've always wanted to see the place. Harvard was founded by a Cambridge man, but I guess you know that.'

'I do.' She looked quizzically at him. 'Were you at Harvard?'

He lowered his cup gently to the saucer. 'I had a semester term, then the Japs bombed Pearl — and here we all are.'

She was pleasantly surprised. 'What were you reading?'

'Law.'

It seemed to please her. 'Really. Is your father a lawyer?'

Bill grinned. 'No — a dentist.'

She feigned mock horror, put a hand to her mouth. 'Oh dear, don't look at mine.'

He couldn't help himself. 'I already have. They're beautiful.'

She pulled a face. 'Nobody's ever said that before.'

But she was inordinately pleased. In the pause that followed he eventually said, 'And your parents, are they academic?'

She giggled.

'Oh dear me no. Dad was a printer but works in an aircraft factory now, and does fire-watching. He was lucky to get home from Dunkirk, though he was badly wounded. Mum looks after the home front and her parents, who are getting on a bit.'

Nodding, he took another sip, looking at her all the time.

'So, aren't you very young to be a fellow?'

'Well, it's the war again isn't it? Shorter degree courses and a lack of people to fill some of the positions.' Her eyes flashed. 'As a woman I've been uniquely lucky. There is no precedent for the position I hold in this all-male college. It's unheard of — so much so that I have to live out. But I was the only one available to fill the gap. The war has changed a lot of things; traditions are under threat — not a bad thing, sometimes.'

He shook his head. 'I think you are being modest.'

'Anyway,' she grunted. 'What exactly do you do in the Air Force?'

'I fly a P51 Mustang.'

She couldn't keep the sudden anxiety out of her voice. 'That's dangerous.'

Bill shrugged. 'Being in a tank or a sub — that's my idea of dangerous.'

They spent another ten minutes talking about nothing in particular, Bill just happy to be in her company, unable to get enough of the sight and sound of her.

She felt the excitement of being with him, began to feel more confident, was conscious of the continuing effect she seemed to be having on him. It was something that she had been aware of with male colleagues, and before that fellow students, but they had not interested her or excited her like this man. It was as if a veil had been removed from her existence. Everything seemed in sharper focus.

With their cups empty they reluctantly got to their feet and made their way slowly back to the porter's lodge.

He turned to her. 'That was really great. I appreciate the time you spent on me.'

It was freezing cold. She began to shiver. 'It was a pleasure. I really enjoyed myself.'

He wanted to wrap his arms around her — keep her warm for ever. Instead he held out his hand. 'Well, I won't detain you any longer.'

She took it. He smiled weakly, held on a fraction longer than he should have. They both knew it. She wasn't unhappy.

At last Bill said: 'Thanks again.'

When he appeared not to be going to say any more she smiled and reluctantly turned to go.

'It was a pleasure.'

She walked away, desperately hoping that he was watching her, that something would happen.

He gazed at her retreating slim figure, his own longing rising with each step she took away from him.

Never had he so wanted to see more of a

girl before. There was just something about her that made him feel good, whole. Emotion suddenly overcame all restraint or shyness.

He called out: 'Hey.'

She stopped immediately and turned, waited.

'Yes?'

He took a deep breath. 'I don't suppose — would you like — ah — can we meet again?'

Her answer nearly blew him away. It also startled her. 'Yes, I'd like that.'

He was disbelieving. 'You would?'

'Yes.'

Bill was so taken aback that he didn't know what to say next. She prompted him.

'Have you any idea when?'

He came to — fast.

'Tonight? I don't suppose you're free tonight for dinner?'

Her face fell. 'Oh dear, I'm booked to dine in college.'

The agony affected them both, then with a deep breath she said: 'I'll make some excuse. Anyway, somebody will get my portion of food.'

Bill brightened up. 'Gee, that's great. What say I come by here at seven? We could eat at my hotel if that's OK with you, then maybe a drink at the Blue Boar or some-where of your choice?'

'Fine. Till then — goodbye.'

Tingling with excitement she walked quickly away, frightened that something might spoil the most terrific, wonderful moment in her life.

Bill watched her go, then turned to leave, and caught the porter looking sternly at him. He gave a huge grin and a high flung salute as he left.

The rest of the afternoon passed quickly. All his well-laid plans went out of the window. He went to the American Red Cross building, managed to buy some nylons from one of the guys before returning to the hotel.

In his room he slipped out of his jacket, kicked off his shoes and flung his tie on to a chair. He'd brought a bottle of Jack Daniel's with him. On the chest of drawers was a tumbler and water-jug. He grabbed the glass, sat on the bed, carefully poured a generous measure, thought about it, poured most of it back, then lay down, head against the board.

What was happening? Less than four hours ago all he could think about was getting back to the job. Now, all he could think about was that moment he first saw her. It was as if an arrow of desire had pierced his heart. He winced; where on earth did that come from? It was like something from a ten-cent girls' magazine. Then he remembered that his eyes had taken in a volume by Blake in the library: . . . *'Bring me my arrows of desire.'*? So it wasn't so corny after all.

Then he had a sudden shocking thought. He didn't even know her first name.

# CHAPTER THREE

The object of his desire was sitting at her dressing-table, an old dressing-gown covering her camiknickers, worried about her first ever date with a complete stranger, one who had aroused such a storm in the previously tranquil ocean of her mind. His name was Bill. She savoured it again. *Bill.*

With a pair of heated tongs she was trying to wave her hair, convinced it wasn't going well. Irritated, she put them down on the stand and looked at herself in the mirror yet again. It would have to do.

She wished she'd paid more attention to clothes and make-up in the past but they hadn't really figured in her interests.

Fortunately she had an old lipstick and some powder her mother had given her, and an eyebrow pencil, which a friend had tried to make her use without success.

She set about her task. When she had finished she contemplated her face from all sides, and felt that she looked like a certain type of woman. Was it the right thing to be doing? She held her nerve, took a pearl-handled hair-brush and did some finishing touches to her hair, then slipped off her dressing-gown. With a large powder-puff she lightly dusted her shoulders and neck with some scented talc.

Her dress she had already selected. It was a simple black affair with a thin belt, gathered sleeves and a V neck, last used when she had received her double first in London. After she had slipped her feet into Cuban-heeled shoes she took a final look at the completed article, then at the clock on the mantelpiece. Time to go.

She drew on her beige coat with its high collar that framed her head, and tightened the belt. The only hat that seemed to go with everything was a black beret with a pom-pom. It had been given to her by a friend who'd bought it when she had toured France in the last year of peace.

She pulled it down one side, tucked some curls in, teased others out until she was as happy as she was going to be with her appearance. The girl who looked back at her from the mirror was a stranger to her.

She took a packed bus into town. It was full of girls going out for the night, chattering and laughing. When she heard them talking about GIs and Yanks she felt herself blushing, almost got off and went home — *almost.* She steadied her nerve with the memory of him, and got to her destination, letting herself in through a side gate and crossing the college paths to arrive at the porters lodge. The porter gave her a startled glance that made her panic.

'Good evening, Doctor Rice.'

'Good evening, Sam.' She smiled uneasily. 'Everything all right?'

He coughed, conscious that his amazement at her appearance had been so obvious. 'Yes, you expecting a taxi, Doctor?'

'No — no, somebody is calling for me.' She glanced up at the clock on the wall behind him, was about to say: 'I'm early,' when the bell clanged as the handle outside the massive oak doors was pulled. She nearly jumped out of her skin.

The porter stepped to the blackout curtain, disappeared behind it as she listened to the small inset door creak open. His voice was immediately recognizable.

'I'm here to meet Doctor Rice.'

'Yes, sir, come in, she's waiting.'

The door shut, then the curtain was pulled aside. Bill stepped into the light, and pulled up as he set eyes on her. 'Wow.'

The porter coughed and waited to let them out. Flushing, she managed: 'Good-evening.'

Bill wanted to whistle — just as the enlisted men would have done. Instead he said: 'You look absolutely marvellous.'

'Thank you.'

Unable to bear the porter's now over-impassive face any more, she said quickly: 'We'd best be going.'

She led the way. With a flourish the porter pulled the curtain behind them, plunging them into pitch blackness, then opened the small inset door. Pale moonlight flooded in.

As soon as they were standing on the cobbles outside the door shut behind them. She had a vague feeling of panic, there was no going back now.

Their faces showed like ghosts, disembod-ied by the dark shadow of the surrounding high wall.

'Here, hang on to my arm.'

Hesitantly she did so. It felt very intimate.

As they walked up the street — darker than it had been in the sixteenth century when the college was new and lit by burn-ing rushes, the porter returned to his lodge. His young assistant, who was spreading lard on to slices of bread, steaming mugs of tea already prepared, said: 'Who'd have thought it — that young Doctor Rice — a Yankee basher.'

The older man snapped: 'Watch yer mouth, young Owen. Doctor Rice is a respected member of the faculty, even though she's a woman.'

But his moustache twitched, and he had to pass a hand across it to hide the grin.

As they walked through the dark streets of Cambridge, with crowds of men shouting and laughing in the tongues of their native countries, but with the accents of the New World dominant, occasional wolf whistles followed her progress, her heels clicking on the pavement.

She hung on to his arm, quite frightened by the reaction she was evoking. By the time he guided her up the steps of the hotel she was acutely aware of the raw biological urge of men who knew they might not be alive the following week.

Inside, in the small foyer, they removed their coats. As they followed the ancient head waiter to their table Bill's eyes wandered over her slim figure with its small waist, shapely legs, and gleaming hair.

He was amazed. He'd been smitten the moment he had set eyes on her, but now, in a totally different way, she was a knock-out.

As they took their seats, the head waiter

holding her chair for her, a small trio in the corner began playing. Couples moved on to the tiny dance-floor.

Bill took the smudged, typed card that passed for a menu, but still only had eyes for her.

He cleared his throat, said nervously: 'That's a wonderful dress.'

At that moment the waiter said: 'The special tonight is fish-pie.'

Nonplussed, they both looked at him for a second, then burst into laughter.

Frowning, the man snapped: 'Is there something wrong?'

Bill eventually managed: 'No — nothing to do with you, it was just the timing. Sorry.'

Huffily the bent-up figure retreated. 'In that case I'll come back in a minute.'

When he'd gone they sat in silence for a second, broken by Bill saying: 'Never did have much success with sweet talk.'

'It was a very nice thing to say.' She'd hardly finished when they both laughed.

'Oh dear.' She found her handkerchief and pressed it to her eye. They studied the cards in silence, both aware that 'nerves' were at the root of it all.

At last, ruefully, Bill said: 'Timing or not, the fish-pie does seem to be the best.'

She agreed. 'Sawdust sausages or stew

with hardly any meat isn't too attractive. I'll have the fish too.'

He took that to be disappointment. Concerned, he said: 'Would you like to try somewhere else — we don't have to stay here?'

She shook her head and laid her menu down. 'Good heavens, no. It's rather nice here. Food is the same everywhere. After nearly five years of war there's not much choice.'

'Maybe I can help you. I can get a few things from the PX.' Even as he offered he knew it was a mistake.

Firmly she declined. 'No — thank you all the same.'

He winced. 'Sorry, coming on the rich Yank, huh?'

She relented. 'No — it's me. It was very generous of you to offer.'

He pleaded. 'Can we forget it?'

She gave a little smile that made him want to grab her and kiss those beautiful lips as they moved.

'Nothing to forget.'

He made a note not to present the nylons tucked in his trench-coat pocket. Not for a while anyway.

The waiter returned with his pencil stub poised above his pad. 'Are you ready to order now?'

Bill spoke for both of them. 'Yes, we're going for the fish-pie — sounds great.'

The pencil stub received a lick before being put to use.

'And to drink, sir?'

'Is there any wine?'

The waiter was triumphant. 'Not any more. The last bottles went Christmas forty-two. We can offer you beer, whisky or water.'

They both looked at her.

'Water for me.'

'Do you mind if I have a drink?' Bill asked.

'Of course not.'

He looked up at the waiter. 'In that case I'll have a glass of your excellent warm beer.'

With a sniff the order was recorded.

'Very good, sir.'

When he was gone she said; 'I think you upset him.'

Bill was regretting it already.

'Yes. Sorry.' He changed the subject, 'Did you get your work done OK?'

'What work?'

Bill emphasized with a hand movement. 'You had some books in the library when I interrupted you.'

She was dismissive. 'Oh that — yes of course.'

'You sound a very determined lady.'

She raised one finely contoured eyebrow. 'My father calls it obstinate.' She looked down into her lap. 'But most of the time I wouldn't say boo to a goose. In fact, I'm really very shy.'

It brought a grunt of sympathy from him. 'And I suppose you won't believe me if I say the same?'

She smiled, and they lapsed into an awkward silence, listening as the band played 'Whispering'.

The drinks came at last. Bill tried to make amends with the old boy.

'That's great. Thank you very much.'

He received a begrudging nod as the man poured water from a jug into Mary's glass before setting it down.

Bill held out his beer and she lifted her tumbler to meet it.

'Cheers.'

She responded: 'Cheers.'

They took sips, then as she set her glass carefully down, she said: 'Lieutenant —'

He interrupted her. 'Bill — please.'

She took a deep breath, conscious that they were going a step further.

'Bill — that's a nice name — is it William, really?'

Hearing her say it for the first time felt really great.

'Yes — but I'm never called that. And you . . . ?' he prompted.

She pulled a face. 'Mary — it's awful, isn't it?'

Bill looked at her intently. 'I think it's a beautiful name.'

She giggled nervously. 'You know what this makes us?'

He looked blank, so she added: 'Do you know your English Kings and Queens?'

'Sure know George the Third — he lost a colony.'

She gave him a stern look but said: 'William and Mary.'

'Ah.' He pretended he understood, but whether she'd meant it or not, the implication that they were a couple was great.

Embarrassed, she felt the same, was amazed that she'd come out with it. Was some unseen force taking charge of her?

'Anyway *Mary* . . .' saying it aloud was wonderful. '. . . what were you about to say?'

She was perplexed for a moment, then remembered. 'Oh yes, what are you going to do after all this has finished? Will you take up your studies with the law again?'

He looked down into his beer. 'Who knows. I'm not the same person any more — none of us are, I guess. I'll just have to take that one when it comes along. Anyway, we all expect to be sent to the Pacific when European operations end.' He shifted in his chair. 'And what about you? Is this going to be your life's work, here in Cambridge?'

Mary shook her head.

'Good heavens, *no*. When the men return no doubt I'll be overlooked for posts, anyway I'd like to do something out of the ordinary for a while — combine some research with working in one of those kibbutzim the Jews are setting up in Palestine. After that . . .' she shrugged her shoulders, 'if I'm not married I suppose a career in academia somewhere, or the Civil Service.'

Bill played his finger slowly around the rim of his glass. 'I have some Jewish blood.'

Puzzled, Mary put her head to one side, quizzed: 'Does that matter?'

'To some — maybe. It certainly didn't to my paternal grandfather — he came from Scotland, by the way. He met my German-Jewish grandmother on the boat over. That's America for you, the great melting-pot of the Western world.'

Mary thought, so *that's* where the knock-out dark hair and blue eyes come from.

Just then the meal arrived. As the waiter and a young girl delivered the fish pie and served some over-cooked sloppy vegetables, they were both glad of a rest from talking, conscious they had known each other barely eight hours in total. This time last night she had gone to bed early to keep warm, and he'd been in the bar.

The day before he'd been over Germany, she at Bletchley reading transcripts purportedly from a German command-centre on the Eastern front. Neither of them had known of the existence of the other.

With the meal, conversation became easier and when they both declined the tapioca pudding, Bill fished out his silver cigarette-case, a present from his parents when he'd won his wings.

He offered her one, was a little surprised when she took it. He applied his lighter to the end.

'I thought maybe you might disapprove.'

Mary blew smoke into the air. 'Thanks. I didn't smoke before the war, but everybody does now. You feel you're not one of the girls if you don't join your mates in a fag.'

Bill chuckled out loud.

Mary frowned. 'What's funny?'

'Old languages you might be good at, but English as she is spoken in the New World, now that's a different proposition, Mary.'

She realized that there was obviously a different connotation to the slang word for cigarette, but only wrinkled her nose at him.

The band struck up a Glenn Miller number — *Moonlight Serenade.* There was a rush to the floor. They watched as the British couples circled the outside, while the Americans shuffled on the spot in the centre.

'Do you like dance music?' Bill asked.

She tapped the end of her cigarette above the ashtray. 'Yes, I do. Got used to it because of the wireless. It's played non-stop all over the place, especially in factories and work places. I haven't had much experience of the real thing though.' Mary winced apologetically and added: 'Bit of a bluestocking, really.

That puzzled Bill. 'Bluestocking?'

Mary saw her chance to tease. 'English as she is spoken in the mother country. It now means a bookworm — a swot — but was originally named after eighteenth-century society hostesses who wore blue hosiery and held the most intellectual soirées in town.'

He frowned mockingly. 'Really. But do you know Glenn Miller?'

She did, but enjoying the banter said: 'Glen who? Is that in Scotland?'

Bill knew he was being strung along, and joined in with relish.

'Who's Glenn Miller? My God, woman, where have you been? You must be one hell of a *green*stocking.'

Mary chuckled. '*Blue.* It's blue as you very well know. Of course I've heard of him. They've broadcast concerts he's given from Bedford — that's not far away. He's stationed there.'

'Yeah?' Bill leaned forward. 'There's a big poster in the Red Cross Club. He's playing at the Guildhall here in Cambridge — would you like to go — it's tomorrow?'

Mary was obviously taken aback. 'Well, I. . . .'

Bill realized what he had done, and panicked. 'I'm sorry. I didn't mean to crowd you. I guess I got carried away.'

Quickly she said: 'Oh, it's not that. It's just — well — I don't know how to dance. I've never done it.'

Bill leapt up and held out his hand. 'Nothing to it. Come on, I'll show you.'

Flustered, but unable to refuse his hand, she stood up. She was still protesting as he led her to the floor.

Mary knew that they were about to come physically very close together. Her heart started to thump against her ribcage.

Bill towed her through the side-stepping quarter-turning British and reached the other Americans shuffling on the spot in the middle. It happened in one smooth movement — Bill just turned back on his tracks as she kept on coming, walking right into him. He slipped his arm around her waist and pulled her closer. Instinctively she placed her left hand on his shoulder.

Breathlessly, Mary warned: 'But I don't know any steps.'

As they shuffled around she slowly relaxed. Her body had been as stiff as a board but she found herself softening, leaning in against his muscular frame, swaying to the music.

'There — you got it. Easy, huh?' Bill encouraged her.

She would never forget *Moonlight Serenade.*

The rest of the evening they were hardly off the floor, eventually clinging heavily to each other as they moved to the slow beat of the double-bass. Her eyes were closed when the music came to an end, and the band-leader, in his dinner-jacket and winged collar pulled the mike nearer.

'That's it tonight, ladies and gentlemen. We hope you have enjoyed yourselves with us, and don't forget, we shall be here again Saturday — same time, same place. . . .'

Obviously in a hurry the band struck up *God Save the King* before he'd quite finished. They stood motionless, but their hands stayed locked tightly together. When it ended there was desultory clapping. They walked back to their table, only relinquishing their grip on each other when the main lights came on.

She looked at her watch. 'Gosh, is that the time? My landlady will be locking up in half an hour, I'll have to hurry.'

He was disappointed. 'Oh, I thought we might have a nightcap — tea or a coffee or whatever.'

Upset, Mary clutched his arm. 'I'm so sorry. But if I do have to be let in, the dean gets a report.' She scowled. 'Only me of course, because I'm a woman at their college. Honestly, with women in munition factories and the like, it's such a nonsense.'

He frowned. 'But your college is only just round the corner.'

Vigorously she shook her head.

'Yes, but I told you before: I live in rooms further out. It will take me all my time in the blackout to get there.'

Anxiously, Bill said: 'You will let me escort you — won't you?'

Her heart started to pound again at the thought of what might happen, but she heard herself saying: 'I was rather hoping you would.'

With their coats on they stepped out through the darkened doorway. A stray shaft of light showed the anti-blast paper criss-crossing the windows, before it was quickly smothered.

Mary's hand found his. 'Careful. Watch out for lampposts. There's many a black eye caused by walking into them — or so they say.'

She led the way, crossing the road and then walking down a lane.

'My place is on the other side of the Cam.'

The dark soaring shapes of the colleges stood out against the starry sky, the Milky Way shining like a bright band of diamonds.

Mary looked up, the faint light catching her upturned face. 'Isn't it wonderful? Since the blackout the night sky has been terrific. We haven't seen the like since the last century — before gas-lamps and electricity in towns.'

Bill looked at her, breathed: 'Yeah — beautiful.'

It happened easily, naturally. Their faces drew closer. At the last moment her eyes closed and their lips brushed, separated, came back again, and stayed.

When at length they parted she put her head against his chest, face sideways, lost in the shadow. His hand gently stroked her hair.

It was a few seconds before she spoke in a

tiny voice.

'Bill, what's happening? This time yesterday we didn't even know each other.'

He kissed her sweet-smelling hair. 'I know. I can't believe it myself.'

They stood for what seemed ages until he said: 'I've got six more days, Mary. Can I see you every day? Can I see you tomorrow? The Glenn Miller show is on at the Guildhall. Now you can dance it would be fun.'

His voice was pleading.

Mary was elated, then suddenly despondent.

'Yes, yes of course. Oh — damn.'

'What's wrong?'

'The day after that is one of my war effort days. In the evening I've got to travel to . . .' Shocked that she nearly said Bletchley Park she stopped abruptly, then ended lamely: 'somewhere for a couple of days.'

Bill's face showed his desperation. 'Must you go? I've only got this week.'

Mary thought furiously. 'I'll call in sick — first thing in the morning. They'll want a note from my doctor, but I'll sort that out somehow. Anyway, I'll catch up later. But I have to give a lecture in the morning — and a tutorial in the afternoon. I can't dodge them, but I'll be free from about four o'clock onwards.'

Bill threw his arms around her and gave her a hug, lifting her feet off the ground as he described a circle before setting her down. 'That's great.' Laughing and joking they moved on — to be blinded by two flashlights catching them full in the face. A voice commanded:

'Stay there, please.'

Two figures stepped up close, the lights dropping to take in their bodies before coming to rest on their chests. The light reflected back so that they could make out two policemen, a sergeant and a constable, with steel helmets and gas-masks on shoulder-straps. The sergeant spoke again.

'Out late, aren't we?'

Bill frowned. 'Just showing the lady home, officer — is there a problem?'

The constable strolled around behind them, examining them with his torch.

Sergeant said: 'No — not that I know of.'

His light fell on to Bill's uniform.

'Can I see both of your identity cards please?'

Mary fiddled in her handbag, lit up by the returned constable's light, while Bill unbuttoned his coat and fished inside his tunic for his wallet, then handed over the card.

The sergeant studied it intently. 'You on

leave, sir?'

'Yep.'

'Have you got your leave pass with you?'

Bill frowned, and began to undo his coat, revealing more of his jacket as he tried various pockets.

'I may have left it at the hotel — I'm staying at the Swan — they needed it for registration. . . .'

Mary found her card and held it out. 'Here we are. I work at the college.' She indicated the high wall they were passing.

The sergeant took it, scanned it, then gave it back. 'Thank you.'

He turned back to Bill, who was still searching his pockets. 'That's all right, sir, that won't be necessary.'

Bill stopped. 'That's very kind of you, I appreciate it.'

The sergeant eased his chinstrap. 'Least I can do, sir. You're doing your bit, I'm sure.'

Bill shrugged. 'We're all doing that, sergeant.' He began to button his coat up again as the sergeant turned to Mary. He was still a bit suspicious.

'And what did you say you did at this college, miss?'

Mary raised an eyebrow, clearly irritated yet again at the incredulity of all men.

'I didn't, sergeant. I'm a research fellow,

and yes I do know it's unusual.'

The policeman was surprised, and couldn't hide it. 'A lady! I see. Very well then, I'll wish you both good-night and good luck.'

They answered in chorus: 'Good-night,' and moved on, her arm in his.

Bill whispered: 'I don't think he believed you.'

Mary grunted. 'From the look on his face I think he thought I ought to be still chained to the kitchen sink.'

When they were out of earshot the constable murmured: 'She's a looker. Bloody Yanks get all the best women.'

His sergeant turned on his heel and began pacing towards town again. 'Did you see his medals?'

The constable snorted. 'They get them for just being here, don't they?'

The sergeant shook his head. 'He's got a DFC, they don't give *them* out willy nilly, I can tell you. So he deserves anything he can get in my book.'

After Silver Street bridge, Mary started down the sandy path which in the moonlight looked to him like his own yellow brick road. He put his arm around her shoulder, and Mary responded by holding on to his waist.

They walked in silence until she said; 'I'm afraid you'll have to go back the long way round.'

He squeezed her shoulder. 'I'm not tired.'

'Neither am I.' She took a deep breath. 'I don't think I'll sleep a wink — I've had such a lovely time.'

Bill kissed the side of her head. 'Me too.'

Later, as they turned into her road of three-storey terrace houses, an increasing roar began to fill the heavens. He felt her shiver, so he stopped and drew her into him and held her tightly.

'It's the RAF — Round The Clock. Now the Army boys are over there, Fortress Europe is nearly finished.'

Her voice came up from his chest. 'What will you be doing when your leave is up?'

He was evasive. 'Oh, back on the job.'

She pulled away and looked up at him. 'Look, Bill, I'm not daft. Tell me what you do *exactly* — if you can — it matters a lot to me.'

Bill thought for a moment. 'OK. I'm in a fighter squadron. We escort bombers.' Her face fell. With a sigh, she said, 'I had hoped that, perhaps, you weren't in the fighting; liason or something like that.'

He pulled her close again, cuddled her. 'It's not like the bomber boys. Compared to them it's a piece of cake.' If she hadn't felt so miserable, she would have chuckled at his use of RAF slang.

He didn't say anything about the targets of opportunity.

The word had come down to strafe airfields on the way home — any aircraft destroyed would now be credited as kills. It made sense, but airfields were heavily defended. . . .

They walked in silence until they reached the gate to her digs.

Bill was anxious. The roar in the sky had diminished to a distant hum, but it was still casting a shadow over the end of the evening.

'You all right? You've gone quiet.'

'Yes.' She did not intend to tell him that her brother had died in the Battle of Britain. He'd got his wings, and three weeks later his Hurricane had gone down in the Channel after his first dogfight. She'd sworn then that she would never get friendly with anybody in the services — especially the Air Force.

She reached up and hugged him. 'Yes — of course.'

It was finding out the precarious reality of their situation that gave her the urge, but she kissed him passionately on the mouth.

She pulled back, said: 'I'll see you tomorrow then — say seven o'clock at the hotel?'

He pleaded: 'No — I'll pick you up here at, say, six-thirty. We had better get there early, it's going to be crowded.'

She frowned, was going to say that her landlady, Mrs Chick, wouldn't approve, and then thought: *damn it,* and said: 'I look forward to it.'

With that she gave him an affectionate peck on the cheek, turned and ran up the stairs and opened the door. Just as she closed it behind her she waved with her fingers.

Bill caught sight of a curtain twitching. He stood for a moment in the empty dark street, then walked away as another roaring in the sky started to build.

When she reached her room Mary leaned back against the door, tears rolling down her cheeks as the unlit room reverberated to the same angry sky.

# CHAPTER FOUR

Bill couldn't get to sleep; his mind kept going round and round, full of Mary, of the moment he had first set eyes on her, and every second since then, the way she moved, the way she smiled, her hair, everything.

Somewhere near 2 a.m., just as he lapsed more into unconsciousness than normal sleep, he was suddenly terrified, he couldn't remember her face. The nightmare continued. The more he tried, the more impossible it was. Then, mercifully, oblivion descended.

He came to at eleven o'clock, lying for some time on his side looking at the strange room from that angle, utterly confused. For a while he thought he was back home somewhere.

At last he sat up and saw his uniform jacket draped over a chair. It all came back with a rush, including the awful feeling of not being able to remember how Mary looked, and with that came *guilt.* He could see her now as though she had been etched into his brain. How could he have forgotten? He must get a photograph — that torment could not be repeated.

The fact that the mental exhaustion the flight-surgeon had diagnosed was affecting him never dawned on him.

There was no shower, so he tried the tub. The water was cold, but the quick plunge and brisk rub-down left him tingling with life and excitement at the prospect of seeing her again.

He remembered, rashly, that he'd said he would take her to the Glenn Miller show, which was in town that night. Guessing it might be difficult to get into, he resolved to ask around.

Dressed, he came down the stairs to find a lady with a headscarf on using a hand-pushed carpet-cleaner. She looked up and grinned, the cigarette that was stuck to her lower lip wobbling up and down as she said: 'Oh, hello darling, awake at last.'

Bill apologized. 'Sorry, I don't normally do that.'

She stopped what she was doing.

'I'm afraid breakfast finished long ago, but I can make you a cup of tea and toast. Or, knowing you Yanks like your coffee, you can have that if you prefer.'

Bill suppressed a shudder at the thought.

'No, thank you. I'll get myself something at the American Red Cross Club, I've got to go there as it is.'

He wandered into Cambridge, standing for a while outside her college, trying to imagine her teaching somewhere inside.

At the Red Cross Club he bought a sandwich and coffee, and had a think about that evening. When he'd finished he took his cup and plate back to the counter. The girls in their crisp blouses and neat skirts, with little forage-caps on their heads, were a breath of home, speaking in American accents, one from the Midwest, the other from the Deep south.

He enquired about the Glenn Miller concert and found it was open to all Allied servicemen. The girl from Tennessee gave him a dazzling smile.

'Get there early, Lieutenant — it's the only way — or you can get a ticket, I believe, if you go to the Guildhall beforehand.'

'Gee, thanks for the information.'

It was then that he thought about transportation: it would make it easier to get there early if nothing else. But a car was out of the question — gas was strictly rationed.

But he was a fighter pilot — full of resourcefulness — or supposed to be, wasn't he? And he loved the thought of doing something for her — something that would impress her.

Bill checked which was the nearest base. When told he implored the Southern belle: 'I wonder, could I use your phone, or rather, would you mind calling for me? I need to speak to the adjutant, rather urgently.'

She gave him a guarded look. 'We're not officially allowed to use the phone for personal calls, Lieutenant.'

Bill frowned. 'Oh, this is very official. I promise you.'

She made up her mind and lifted the counter hatch. 'Come on through — the phone is in the office.'

He followed her trim figure into a small, obviously newly partitioned area. She picked up the receiver and ran a hand down a wall chart of bases and other facilities and found the number she wanted.

The finger she used to dial on the rather ancient-looking black phone was well manicured. It finally found the last hole and the disc whirred back.

When she spoke Bill could well imagine her accent was even more noticeable at the other end of the line.

'Hi there, this is the Red Cross Club in Cambridge. Can I have the adjutant's office please. Thank you.'

She placed her hand over the speaker. 'Who shall I say is calling?'

Bill had been thinking furiously, and had come up with the one person that fitted the situation.

'General Myers.'

She nearly dropped the phone, began hissing 'I can't —'

He could hear a voice bark at the other end. Caught out she spluttered:

'I . . . have General Myers for you, sir.'

She shot the phone out to him as though it was red-hot.

Bill took it, made his voice more authoritative and deeper.

'Myers here.' He knew the general to be on leave in the States. 'I'm in Cambridge, staying at the . . .' He put his hand over the receiver, spoke to her. 'What's the best hotel in town?'

Reluctantly she shrugged. 'The University Arms, I suppose.' He repeated it into the phone.

'I need a vehicle for tonight. I'm attending a group conference and my transportation has gone belly-up.'

She listened as he made a few grunting

replies, then: 'I'm much obliged, Major. I'll see that your helpfulness does not go unnoticed. Eighteen thirty hours. That would be fine. Thank you.'

Grinning, he lowered the phone.

She had one fine eyebrow raised, arms crossed, fingers tapping her blouse.

'Lieutenant, I don't know what you're up to, but don't involve me in future — *right?*'

'Right.'

But there was softness in those Southern eyes.

Satisfied with himself he wandered out into the town and found the Guildhall. To his relief he got three tickets.

Bicycles were everywhere, hundreds of students in short gowns were cycling all over the place, mingling with working men in cloth caps carrying haversacks, and women in headscarves, with big wicker baskets hooked to their handlebars over the front wheel. The air was full of the sound of tinkling warning bells, and once he stepped out unthinkingly into the road and was bumped quite badly by a speeding bike, the man shouting something that Bill could only guess was a rebuke as to his not knowing which side of the road civilized people travelled on.

He spent an hour looking into beautiful

Victorian shop-windows, all polished glass and wooden framed, with white canvas sun-blinds drawn down over the sidewalks. But after nearly five years of war, there was very little on display that could actually be bought.

There were a lot of GIs around, some in clusters, others with girls on their arms. The RAF were present, and some servicemen of other nationalities, all wandering aimlessly.

Eventually he found a path that took him down by the river. He sat on a bench, enjoying the weak sun on his face.

He was thinking about what might happen at the end of his leave, how they would manage, when a young voice said: 'Got any gum, chum?'

Startled, he turned to find a boy in short grey trousers and long socks, a blazer with a badge on the breast pocket, and wearing a peaked school cap on his head. He had a satchel on his back.

Bill smiled.

'Shouldn't you be at school?'

The boy grinned, 'Got a free period, just on my way home.'

Bill fished in his pocket and pulled out a fresh pack. 'Here you go, son.'

The boy's face lit up, exposing teeth full of gaps as he caught the packet.

'Gee, thanks, that's great.'

Almost immediately three more boys, all in short trousers, came from nowhere. What was it with the English, putting their kids in short trousers in winter?

He waved them away.

'Hey, that's all I've got this time.'

It was true, he wasn't a big gum fancier, but like many, he always slipped a strip into his mouth before flying at altitude to combat the dry mouth caused by the oxygen.

He turned back to the boy.

'You live round here, son?'

'Yes.' The boy pointed. 'Over there.'

'What's your daddy do?'

'He's in the army.'

Bill pulled his chin in. 'Hey, that's impressive. Is he over in Normandy?'

The boy shook his head. 'No, he's a prisoner of war.'

Bill was taken aback, then remembered Dunkirk. 'Was it when the British had to leave France?'

'Oh no, he's in the Fourteenth Army.'

The boy seemed to think that was sufficient explanation in itself, and was momentarily puzzled when Bill prompted: 'Where are they?'

The boy began to open the gum packet.

'He was taken prisoner in Burma.'

The awful truth dawned on Bill. The boy's father was in a Jap POW camp. He'd heard of the way things were in them. Like most Americans, though Nazi Germany was seen as the primary threat to the US and democracy in the West, there was a special hatred of the Nips — ever since Pearl Harbor. Most servicemen assumed that if they survived the European theatre, they would end up being shipped to the East.

'Gee, I'm sorry about that, son. What's your name?'

'Edward Stevenson, sir.'

'Well Edward, enjoy the gum. Do you get enough to eat?'

'Oh yes. Mum's a really good cook and she gets lots of extra things from Uncle Sam.'

'Uncle Sam?' But understanding was already beginning to dawn.

'Yes. Al brings it. He's one of your lot. You are in the Air Force, aren't you?'

Bill nodded. 'That I am. What does this Al do?'

'He's the boss of something. It's very hush-hush, you know.'

I bet it is, thought Bill, and wondered what the friendship of Mrs Stevenson and Al was doing for Anglo-American relations in the district. Not a lot probably. On embarkation they'd all been given a booklet on how not to offend the natives, but it stood to reason that in a case where a man was in a POW camp, feelings might be running high at a wife going out with a Yank.

Then he thought of the woman, alone, in her early vigorous years with a young son, skimping on food, short of company, short of fun, and worried sick as well.

It was easy to criticize. Men made war, but women suffered.

But then there was Mary. Shouldn't she be going out with a RAF guy? Maybe — but she *wasn't*. And it was different.

He patted the boy on the shoulder.

'Well, you best be getting home. You take care of your mother, now, and tell her not to worry, the Japs will soon have had enough.' He didn't believe that for one minute.

'Yes, sir.' The boy cut an American-style salute as opposed to the British open-palm method, and ran off happily.

Sadly Bill gazed at the sparkling sun-kissed water. There was more misery and suffering to come after this war was over, other than the obvious.

Just then a swan took off from the river, neck straight out, giant wings straining with the effort of getting airborne.

He grunted.

Just like a 'Fort' fully bombed-up and taking off for a mission.

Mary looked at the fresh faces around her, three young men who were not much younger than Bill, but there the similarity ended. Whereas they were still immature, blank canvases on which life had yet to paint, the mantle of war gave Bill a maturity far beyond his tender years. But it would not be long when, with shortened wartime degrees finished, they would be called up, poor things.

She screwed the top back on to her fountain pen. 'Well, that's it for this afternoon.'

They began to fold up their notepads and put them with their text books. Filing out of her study they all said politely: 'Thank you, Doctor Rice.'

They closed the door behind them, leaving her still sitting in the window seat that she favoured for her tutorials — and filled with an infinite sadness.

Where would they be in a year or so? In fact, would they still be alive?

Mary could not suppress a shiver. She knew why she was suddenly anxious. That night she had been thinking about Bill, not getting off to sleep until very late and then seeming to wake every hour or so.

All of a sudden, in the blink of an eye, her whole life had changed.

It defied logic.

And with it had come frightful, bone-deep worry about his safety — she had already lost a brother to the great maw of the war.

So there was an urgency in her blood.

Later, as she prepared yet again to meet him, surveying her half-clothed form in the mirror, her face and neck flushed as vague, half understood ideas began to form, making her even more unsettled.

Downstairs she waited in the hall. Mrs Chick gave her a disparaging look as she came out of the dining-room and went into her own ground-floor room.

After five minutes there was still no sign of him. She looked at herself in the hall mirror. If he failed to turn up after all this preparation she would feel humiliated in front of Mrs Chick and the other girls in the house, not that that would really matter if such a terrible thing happened. But she knew it never would — not Bill.

Ten minutes later she began to wonder if he had come to some sort of harm. It was then that a car pulled up in the road, a door slammed, and footsteps came up the path.

Mary didn't wait for the door-knocker to be used, she opened the door.

To her relief he stood there, cap off, looking pleased and apologetic all at the same time.

'Mary, I'm so sorry I'm late — but my car didn't turn up on time.'

'Your car?' She was incredulous. Nobody had cars — not unless they were very, very important, not even Americans.

He grinned, stepped to one side and gave an exaggerated courtly sweep of his hands to show her the staff car and driver, waiting with the rear door open.

'Your carriage awaits you, madam.'

Mary stepped gingerly out and let him escort her to the grinning driver. She stepped into the leathered interior, noticing that the man gave an appreciative nod to Bill as he said: 'You were right, sir, she was worth it.'

When Bill settled into the seat beside her and the door was closed, but before the driver got into his seat she whispered:

'What's he talking about — she's worth it?'

Bill murmured: 'Tell you later. I've got tickets by the way, but we need to get there as soon as possible.' He found her hand, squeezed it and lowered his voice. 'You look stunning.'

Mary pulled a face.

'I didn't know what to put on.'

His gaze dropped to her knees, exposed as the flared pleated skirt rode up on the shiny seat. He was also aware of the fragrance of the woman next to him. She was so desirable it was painful to be sitting there.

The driver's eyes met his in the rear view mirror. There could be no mistake that he thought so too. When he'd got to the University Arms hotel he'd found a humble Lieutenant with a ticket for the Glenn Miller concert for him — as long as he played along. He'd expected a gruff old general and a long wait at some boring conference. The deal was struck.

They swept into the square. It was jammed with men in uniform and girls, with what seemed scores of white-helmeted American military police and British Redcaps, together with groups of special constables in dark-blue uniforms.

It took ages for the driver to park, there were so many trucks and military buses in town. He got her out of the car, wolf whistles coming from all sides of the road. Bill scowled, but felt immensely proud. Alarmed, Mary clung to him for protection. As they got to the entrance the milling throng was such that he had to put an arm around her shoulders, then around her waist to stop them being separated. Mary was oblivious to the pushing and shoving, the only thing that mattered to her was the feeling of his large hand just above her hip, pinning her to him.

Secure.

Belonging.

*His.*

She was disappointed when he took it away to show his tickets. Inside, the place was heaving, and when they pushed through some double doors it was to be met by a vast army of men in uniform of all types, and girls in varying dresses, standing before the stage listening, swaying and tapping to the music. On stage was the Glenn Miller orchestra, lines of saxophones and trombones catching the overhead light as the musicians stood up and sat down as they played *Little Brown Jug.*

Behind them were two huge flags, one the Stars and Stripes, the other the Union Flag hanging straight down from the roof. They edged further in, the back of the hall was full of dancers, jitterbugging frantically, some of the girls being thrown into the air over the shoulders or through the legs of their partners. Around the edge closest to them couples shuffled on the spot, while above it all, the glass ball hanging from the ceiling sent shafts of reflected light down on to the mass of humanity below that was, for the moment, oblivious to the outside world and its pain and suffering.

'Do you wish to listen, or shall we dance?' he asked. She giggled and pointed. 'I certainly can't do that.'

A girl, spinning like a top to the left, was then snapped by her partner's hand to the right, her skirt flying up to give a flashing glimpse of stocking-tops and underwear, the man's legs kicking one way then another, in time to the beat.

Embarrassed, Bill shook his head.

'No — me neither.'

The band came to the end of *Brown Jug* to roars and clapping, and swung almost immediately into *Tuxedo Junction.*

They began shuffling on the spot, until they were violently jolted, sending her hard into him. He wrapped his arms protectively around her. Mary snuggled into his chest, Bill's face in her hair. They hung on to each other, content at last after a night and a day of frustrated longing. They did not join in shouting 'Pennsylvania Six-Five Thousand,' but were lost in their own little world, even when the music came to an end. When there was a great roar and clapping they reluctantly parted, but still held hands as a man in uniform, wearing rimless glasses and carrying a conductor's baton started to speak into a large flat microphone.

Excited, Bill jerked his head in the man's direction.

'Say that's Glenn Miller.'

She chuckled. 'I thought it might be — it's his band, after all.'

Wincing, he detected the gentle mocking humour in her eyes, and loved it.

'I asked for that.' He pulled her to him with mock roughness. 'We can't all be as bright as some.'

Strangely, after years of being considered self-willed, Mary enjoyed being taken to task.

Glenn Miller said his bit, and to great roars of approval, turned back to the band which broke into *String of Pearls.*

Somehow he didn't have to ask her, Mary just seemed to be in his arms again. It was too noisy to talk, they just danced until they couldn't dance any more, then he led her into the bar to cool down.

'What would you like to drink?'

She waved her hand. 'Anything long and cool. An orange-squash will do.'

He struggled into the mob, pushing his

way to the bar. When he returned she'd been asked twice to dance.

They took their drinks to a shelf and leant against the wall. She fished in her bag and came out with a small packet of five cigarettes.

He accepted one, seeing to hers first with his gun-metal lighter. 'Are you enjoying yourself?'

The end of the cigarette burned brightly as she inhaled, then, blowing out the smoke she said:

'Very much so. Thank you for asking me. And the car — what a lovely surprise.'

There was a twinkle in his eye.

'Couldn't have you walking in your finery.'

Mary frowned. 'Hardly finery.' She indicated the skirt. 'Had this for years.'

From the main hall came a fanfare of trumpets and the orchestra started up again. There was a general rush in that direction.

The bar was left half-empty.

'Maybe we ought to sit this one out?' he suggested.

She nodded. 'If you don't want me to collapse with exhaustion I think it would be a good idea.'

Mary didn't like to admit that her shoes were killing her.

He jerked his head in the direction of a

couple of empty chairs.

'Over there.'

They moved to a table and settled down, spending the next ten minutes talking about the sights and sounds all around them.

'Do you like any other types of music?' she asked.

He scratched his cheek.

'I'm keen on jazz.'

'What about classical?'

Bill chuckled. 'Well, I play a mean piano. You should hear my *Für Elise* — from as far away as possible.'

'Truly?'

He held a hand to his chest.

'Cross my heart and hope to die. My mother made me do all my grades.'

Mary sat back, shaking her head in mock disbelief.

'I'm not sure you're telling me the truth.'

Bill threw his arms wide. 'Would I lie?'

Mischievously she passed the tip of her tongue over her upper lip.

'Maybe — how would I know?'

'I'll prove it. Where's a piano?'

Mary looked anxiously around.

'Oh no, not now, I believe you — truly.'

He enjoyed her obvious English embarrassment at the thought of a public fuss.

'Well, when?'

Mary smiled, put her head to one side, arched an eyebrow quizzically and said 'Next time?'

He felt a rush of excitement.

But his euphoria was short lived. Somehow they got on to flying, and she became withdrawn, quiet.

Mary had been forced to remember the reality of their position. Sometime next week he would be over Nazi Germany in the thick of it again, and she, of all people, knew the terrible price to be paid. It frightened and horrified her. She just shouldn't be there, with him, getting to know him — getting closer.

Abruptly she stood up.

'Let's go back in.'

He followed, not taking his eyes off her shining hair as it swished around her firmly held shoulders, aware that something was wrong, and only guessing that it was to do with flying.

But when she turned, putting up her arms for him to take hold of her, the warmth was back in her eyes. Relieved, he took hold of her, drew her into him with a firmness that came from a growing assurance.

Her body crushed against his as her breath came out in a little rush.

But she hung on, didn't complain as they

jostled and moved to the rhythm of all the great hits he knew so well from the radio.

Later the mood changed, to slow smoochy numbers. She slid her hands up his chest over his shoulders and around his neck, touching his hair. His hands met in the small of her back, holding her outstretched body against his.

The tenor's soft voice breathed out the words above the muted saxes: *'At last, my love has come along, my lonely days are over. . . .'*

She lifted her head and looked expectantly at him.

They were still kissing when the song ended, oblivious to all around them.

The band finished the evening with a specially scored rendition of the Army Airforce Battle Hymn. A thousand voices sang, clapped and whistled *'Off we go into the wild blue yonder, climbing high into the sky. . . .'*

Bill guided her to the door. They ran down the steps into a square that was, if anything, even more crowded than before. Military and civil police had doubled as the pubs were coming out at the same time. There was the sound of smashing glass as a fight started up a side street.

Bill was more assertive as he hurried her to the car. 'Let's get the hell out of here.'

More wolf whistles followed their progress. At the car the driver was already there, together with a very large military policeman. He saluted Bill, but couldn't take his eyes off Mary, holding the door for her as she got in, forgetting to check how come Bill had the use of a staff car.

The driver started the engine and waited as the MP held up a bus and then waved them away.

She giggled as he saluted again.

'Bill, will you get into trouble for this?'

The driver answered. 'No miss, they'll never know. And thank you for the ticket sir — the boys won't believe me.'

Bill grinned, putting his arm around her shoulders as she snuggled up to him to keep warm.

'Think nothing of it.'

As they drove slowly out of the town centre through the blacked-out streets, the headlights reduced by masking tape to narrow slits, she leant her head on his shoulder. They didn't speak, content to be just close.

But when at last they turned into her road she suddenly sat up. 'Driver, would you stop here.'

As the car drew to a halt a worried Bill said: 'You OK?'

She nodded. 'The old witch will be waiting up, listening. This way I can get in and up the stairs before she knows it.'

The driver started to get out to open her door, then found Bill's eyes in the rear-view mirror which had lit up. There was no doubting the message. He coughed. 'Do you mind if I step out for a cigarette, sir?'

Bill nodded his thanks. 'Carry on — five minutes.'

When he'd gone Bill gently placed the palm of his hand on the side of her face and turned her head to him, finding her lips with his own. The kiss was long, the most passionate they had ever shared.

Eventually his hand dropped to the outside of her thigh, under her coat which had fallen open. Mary stiffened, felt as if hot blood had surged into her belly. His hand moved higher, pulled tighter so that her hips turned. Her bottom almost left the seat as she was pressed harder against him. Through the thin material of her dress Mary realized that he was reacting to the feel of her, and she knew that something inside her had been set in motion, something which she had never experienced before, something exquisitely unstoppable, unless. . . .

Fear of the unknown made her pull herself free. 'Sorry, I've got to go.'

She started to open the door. Flustered,

he jumped out and ran around to her. 'Mary, I'm sorry. Have I upset you?'

She smiled and placed a hand on his arm. 'No, there's nothing to worry about — I promise. It's been a wonderful evening.'

'You'll see me tomorrow?' he pleaded.

'Of course, it's what I want. I'll come to you.'

'What time?'

She thought for a second.

'How about first thing?'

His face broke into a beam.

'Come early — early as you can.'

She chuckled. 'I'll be at your hotel around nine — all right?'

Bill's smile grew even wider.

'Great. I'll be waiting.'

They looked searchingly at each other, their faces caught in the pale light of a half-moon.

In the seconds that elapsed, more was said then than with a thousand words of love. She suddenly went up on her toes, gave him a peck on the cheek, and walked quickly away.

Bill stood looking after her until she was lost in the shadows.

In bed, when she'd stopped shivering and warmed up, Mary thought again of the overwhelming, frightening urge she had had in the car — like being on the edge of a precipice.

She shivered again, but this time not with the cold. It took only a second or two for her to realize what she had to do — what she *wanted* to do, but the rest of the night was spent in a restless half-awake, half-asleep torment at the magnitude of what she was thinking; of jumping over the edge into the abyss.

In the morning, when she was dressing, Mary looked down at her body.

Taking a deep breath she realized she was saying farewell to innocence.

# CHAPTER FIVE

Bill was waiting for her on tenter-hooks. Every time the phone rang at reception he tensed up. By 9.30 he was pacing up and down and continually going to the door. Eventually, to his immense relief, he saw her coming up the steps, looking fresh and wholesome and wonderful.

He rushed out to meet her. 'Hi.'

She paused, smiled up at him. 'Good morning. Did you sleep all right?'

'No — you?'

'No.'

They grinned ruefully at each other, then she became serious.

'Bill, can we have a coffee? I need to say something — while I'm clear-headed and resolute.'

Anxiety descended on him like a ton weight. 'What's the matter?'

Mary suddenly realized from his face that he was suspecting all sorts of things.

'Oh no — I just need to — well, talk.'

He took a deep breath. 'Right. Shall we have it here?'

'No, there's a place round the corner I use.'

They walked together, not touching, through a street of people in drab, shabby clothing, past a torn poster exhorting the populace to 'Dig for Victory'.

The place she led the way into was a narrow 'hole in the wall' with a serving counter, a couple of tables in the back, and a row of stools facing a shelf.

The man operating the big tea-urn gave her a friendly greeting. 'Morning, miss. The usual?'

She waved her hand in Bill's direction. 'Two coffees please, Mr Archer, I've got company today.'

As she led the way to one of the wooden tables Bill got the distinct impression that Mr Archer was surprised by his presence — to say the least.

They sat down, said nothing as they waited while the proprietor prepared the coffees. He turned and held them out. Bill started to get up but Mary put her hand on his shoulder as she beat him to it.

'Let me.'

Bill subsided back into the chair, feeling

increasingly uneasy.

With the cups set down on the table he waited.

She took a sip, seemed to be steeling herself.

He could bear it no longer. 'Well?'

Mary glanced up at him, then away again. She'd been agonizing all night, and had come to a decision.

'Are we — is this — well for me it seems very special, but for all I know this is just what people experience all the time. . . .'

Bill felt tremendous elation.

It just came out.

'Mary, I love you.'

She searched his face. Slowly it dawned on her that what he had said was sincere — was really *meant.*

She took a deep breath, let out the air slowly. 'That's good. Because I love you so much — and it's happened so suddenly — so fiercely. I just had to know . . . had to hear you say it. I was frightened that it was me — I'm not very experienced in these things — well, actually, I've had *no* experience at all.' She hung her head down in embarrassment.

Bill leaned forward, kissed her gently on the forehead. 'I'm glad you did. I've been so worried that I was going to make a fool of myself, that you would think I was just another Yank on the make.'

Mary smiled weakly, her hand finding his. 'I'd *never* think that.'

They drank in silence for nearly a minute, conscious of a turning point, of a new closeness.

He was just about to ask her what she would like to do when Mary swallowed hard and said: 'Bill?'

'Yes.' He wondered what was coming next.

She'd gone red, found it hard to look at him directly. 'Only if you agree of course, but I've a friend . . .' She paused, took a deep breath, then finished with a rush . . . 'who has a little cottage in the country, miles from anywhere. She's not using it so I wondered if you'd . . . if you'd . . . ?'

She couldn't get it out. Her face seemed to be on fire.

Bill suddenly understood. He set his cup down, found both her hands and made her turn towards him. To be absolutely sure, concerned that he'd got it wrong, he gently asked: 'Mary, is that to stay — tonight?'

Silently she nodded. There was no mistaking her intent. He leant forward, kissed her gently on her forehead.

'I love you.'

She looked down into her lap.

'I know.'

Relieved but still shaking she brightened up. 'To get there we bike — that's if you can ride one?'

He pulled his chin into his chest in a manner, she realized, reminiscent of Cary Grant.

'I practically grew up with a bike between my legs. Lead me to it.'

Mary came right back to her normal efficient self.

'Good. But first I've got some shopping to do. I've got my ration book with me.'

Bill was careful. 'Can I help there?'

Sheepishly, Mary put a hand on his arm. 'I was being silly last night. Of course you can — but we'd better get started, there will be queues at the butcher's by now.'

'Queues — what are they?'

Not sure whether she was having her leg pulled she prompted: 'Outside shops and cinemas. You must have seen them?'

Enlightenment dawned. 'Ah, standing in line, taking your turn. Right.' He frowned. 'How say we go to my sources first — see what they can do?' He tempted her with: 'Might save time?'

She relented, grinned. 'All right.'

They finished their coffee and stood up.

He waited as she pulled her coat back on, helping her find her sleeve. She found his attention very nice, very comforting.

She turned and said: 'Thank you.'

When she'd picked up her bag he said: 'Mary.'

She paused, looked up at him questioningly. 'Yes?'

He took her face in his hands and very very gently kissed her on the lips.

'Lest there be any doubt.'

A couple of hours later they were clear of Cambridge, cycling along a lane, sometimes holding hands, wobbling along, once nearly going into each other as two Mosquitoes passed hedge-high, the sudden deafening roar of their engines gone as quickly as it had come.

They arrived at a crossroads and dismounted.

'Which way?' he asked as Mary looked uncertainly in all directions. Half-turning the front wheel to the right she said: 'I think we go — this way.'

'You don't sound too sure. Don't they signpost anything around here?'

She spun her pedal around backwards until it was in the right position to push off. 'They were all taken down during the invasion scare.'

Suddenly she nodded to a track that ran

off the lane into a wood. She seemed to make up her mind.

'Come on, that's it.'

As she sped off he followed, wobbling with the weight of his pannier bags.

'Hey, hang on, wait for me.'

Giggling she raced ahead and turned down the track. Almost immediately her front wheel caught in a rut. She screamed as she went over the handlebars and into a hedge. Bill caught up, laying his bike on the ground and rushing over to her all in one non-stop motion.

Concerned, he knelt beside her. 'Are you hurt?'

Mary rolled on to her back, got her breath back and looked up at him. 'No — just my pride.'

He grinned his relief, and tweaked her nose. 'Serves you right, leaving me behind.'

He stood up, held out his hands. 'Come on, I'm dying to see this cottage.'

He put a foot either side of her and hauled her to her feet, then helped her brush off twigs and mud. Mary smacked his hand away as he paid too much attention to her bottom. 'That's enough, thank *you.*'

Grinning, he retrieved her bicycle, checked it out, standing with both legs either side of the front wheel as he straightened the handlebars.

Mary picked up the spilled contents of her wicker basket.

They resumed their journey but not quite so fast. Another quarter of a mile along the track widened, the wood ended, and there was a thatched cottage with a pond and ducks. From a gate a gravelled path led to the oak front door.

Mary looked at the sign, half buried in the hedgerow and read it aloud: 'Keeper's Cottage — that's it.'

He looked around and whistled. 'Hey, this is great.'

Mary nodded. 'It's very picturesque, I must say.'

They leant their bikes against the fence and opened the gate. It gave a creak.

Under the porch Mary lifted a flower-pot and produced an old iron key. The lock turned easily but she could not budge the door. Bill leant over her and pushed with the flat of his hand. It flew open.

They stepped into a low-beamed room with, on the far side, french windows, beyond which they could see a small paved terrace with a white iron table and two chairs.

There was a brick fireplace, and opposite it a glass twenties-style cocktail cabinet tucked in under a dog-leg staircase. A sofa and two chairs were grouped around the hearth, and a floor-standing wireless and gramophone was under the little lattice window beside them.

A steady clunk-clunk came from a grandfather clock.

Enchanted, Bill took a step forward.

'Say, this is swell — *ouch!*'

His head connected with a heavy oak beam.

Mary winced and went to him. 'You all right? You Americans are so tall.'

'It hurts.' He rubbed the spot.

Mary lifted her hands to his head. 'Let me see.'

She gave it a rub and a peck.

'You'll live.'

He brought in the string shopping-bags of food and cartons of cans to Mary, who had opened the french doors to air the room, and was now in the very basic kitchen, looking into the scullery beyond with its boiler and mangle. She shut the door firmly on them. 'Well, I'm *not* going to use that room this visit.'

When he returned with her week-end case and his bag, and set them down at the foot of the stairs, she was on her knees at the grate, filling it with tightly rolled nuggets of twisted newspaper, topped with some kindling.

He strode to her, seized her around the waist and lifted her away. In a mock Red Indian voice he said: 'Making fire — *man's* work.'

Mary gave him a box of Swan Vestas along with a pained look. 'Right Big Chief — carry on. I'll get the kitchen straightened out.'

Bill lit a match — set it to the paper. It took very slowly then seemed to go out. He tried somewhere else, the paper charring but never bursting into flame. He was still concentrating on it when the heat from the burnt out match reached his skin.

'Ouch.' He shook his hand vigorously to fan it cool.

Mary, in the kitchen giggled at the yell and took a peek.

He lit another one, tried somewhere else, with only marginally better results. It slowly smoked. He called out: 'This is never going to work. There's no draught.'

Mary made a face, closed a cupboard and returned to the sitting-room.

She shook her head pityingly. 'Don't you have open fires in America, Sitting Bull? Here — give me one of those.'

He passed her a newspaper. Mary opened

it out. 'Move aside.'

Bill got out of the way as she spread it over the mouth of the fireplace, pinning it at the top corners and holding it in the middle of the bottom edge with her foot.

She spoke over her shoulder. 'This is what you do.'

Immediately a draught started up the chimney, sucking the paper inwards so that she had to hold it tightly.

Bill saw the roaring glow that shone through the paper.

'Hey, that's brilliant.'

She jerked her head in his direction.

'Come and take over.'

He crouched over her, taking the corners first, then getting his foot next to hers to replace it as she ducked away.

Mary made for the stairs, picked up her week-end case and climbed the twisting steps. It was dark at the top. She opened a wooden door with its latch, to be confronted by a small bathroom. The iron bath on claws and balls was water-stained, the taps corroded. She tried one. It wouldn't turn. The other did, but nothing came out of it. She frowned, turned her attention to the wash bowl. Ice-cold water roared from one tap and trickled out of the other.

There was only one other door on the tiny

landing. She opened it. Apart from a very small oak wardrobe and a kidney-shaped dressing-table, a large double bed filled most of the room. It was covered in a padded eiderdown, and had a dark, brooding headboard of carved mahogany.

Mary stared at it, feeling suddenly weak at the knees. This was where. . . .

*It* would happen.

She put her case down, and tentatively sat on the edge of the bed. The springs gave such a groan that her nerves overcame her and she fled.

As she came hurriedly down the stairs he turned in consternation to look at her. She paused, hand to her throat.

But before he could say anything, she suddenly started to laugh.

Bill frowned. 'Hey! What's so funny?'

She pointed at him, but he had already started to feel the heat. He spun around and yelled as his hands were caught in the fireball that had been the paper. Bill jumped around, stamping at the fiery remnants.

Mary suppressed her chuckles and nodded at the roaring fire in the grate. 'Well, you certainly got that going.'

Later, in the kitchen, after a cup of tea, they prepared the vegetables for the evening meal. When everything was done Mary wiped down the table.

'Right, that's finished. What do you want to do now?'

Bill put an arm each side of her, and gripped the table, trapping her against it.

'How about this?'

He found her lips with his own. Mary responded, her hands sliding up his back.

After a while she broke off, and gently pushed him away. 'Bill, let's go for a walk before it gets dark.'

He smiled.

'Sure. It's beautiful around here.'

She wrapped a thick country coat around her, which she had found on a hook on the back door and they set off, feet crunching on the gravel until they reached the track. She led the way, nimbly climbing a stile.

Tentatively he broke the quiet that had descended on them. 'It's a lovely evening.'

She slipped her arm through his and squeezed, which made him feel better.

'Yes.'

He grinned down at her. 'Feels good — like we're an old married couple.'

Mary flinched, took a deep breath. 'Bill, I spent a sleepless night, agonizing about — about tonight. I want to — truly I do.'

She tried again. 'You must believe me —

but, well, to tell the truth I'm a bit frightened. . . .'

Mary swallowed hard and continued 'I haven't done anything like this before.' Feeling wretched she added: 'I'll probably be hopeless.'

Bill stopped, drew her into him. 'If you mean what I think you mean — neither have I.'

She was incredulous. '*You* haven't?'

'No.'

Mary shook her head in disbelief. 'But you're *American!*'

Ruefully he chuckled. 'I had a very sheltered New England upbringing.'

'Oh.'

She seemed relieved. 'We're both — *new, then?*'

Embarrassed, he admitted: 'Yes.'

They resumed walking in silence. Bill glanced across at her. She seemed deep in thought, suddenly stirring to say: 'I'm going to dress up for dinner — make an effort to be, well — *special.*'

'You don't have to.'

Mary shook her head fiercely. 'I do. I want it to be right — just as if we were on our honeymoon.'

He protested. 'But I've only got my uniform.'

'That's just fine. It's the woman's place to be — well as nice as possible for her husband.'

'Aw honey — don't worry about that. Anyway, where are you going to get more clothes from?'

Mary looked slyly up at him. 'I asked my friend. She said I could borrow what she's got here. We're the same size.'

He stopped in his tracks. 'I've got a hell of a lot to learn about you. So, would it be in order for me to give you some nylons now?'

Mary teased. 'Oh, so that's all I'm worth is it — a pair of nylons, eh?'

He protested. 'No — no. I didn't mean it like that!'

She poked him in the ribs, and said in mock cockney: 'I'm rather thrilled — it's naughty — taking nylons from a Yank.'

He gave her a gentle slap on the behind. 'Good-time girl.'

Mary reached up and pulled his head down to her.

They kissed and she took his hand.

'Come on, let's go back.'


Bill, looking spruce in his freshly pressed and brushed uniform, put another log on the fire and slapped his hands together to clean them.

Mary's voice carried down the stairs. 'Fix yourself a drink.'

He made for the cocktail cabinet. 'OK. You want one?'

'Not just now, thank you.'

Bill checked out the bottles, found a whisky and poured a generous measure.

He called up the stairs. 'We got any ice?'

She sounded exasperated. 'No *we do not.* Drink it neat like the natives — room temperature, maybe with a little cold water.'

Grumbling, Bill took a sip, sniffed, took another sip, then poured some more. He moved to the gramophone, found a pile of records and sorted through them.

'Hey, there's some Glenn Miller records — can we play them?'

From the room above came: 'Of course.'

He slipped one from its cover, placed it on the turntable, then lowered the arm to the undulating black surface.

A trumpet broke the silence.

Upstairs, Mary sat before the tiny dressing-table, her black petticoat straps dimpling her pale slim shoulders, her dark wavy hair brushed down close to one eye, like Pat Roc in one of her films.

By the light of two candles, one either side of the mirror, she applied a deeper than usual red lipstick which she had found in the drawer.

When she had finished, Mary sat back. A little shiver ran through her. There was no doubting the intent of the woman reflected back at her.

Mary's blood seemed to be thumping around in her body. She stood up, thrust out one shimmering leg, cupped her hands around the wonderfully smooth nylon, and drew it up to tighten the seam at the back until she reached the top.

Her suspender was black, and contrasted with the white soft skin of her thigh. She did the same for the other.

From the wardrobe she took out a taffeta dress cut on the bias, stepped in and buttoned it up. With her shoes on she swung from side to side, making the material rustle seductively. Her tummy seemed to be floating free inside her.

Mary took a deep breath, touched her tongue nervously to her lips, and whispered to herself: 'Here we go.'

He was sipping his drink, foot tapping to the rhythm of the music, and looking into the fire. He heard her heels on the stairs and turned.

Mary knew immediately that she had achieved the desired effect. He was speechless. She came down to the last but one step, gave a twirl, knowing that she was flaunting herself.

He caught a glimpse of a stocking top, and above, something lacy.

She came to rest, hands on hips.

'Well?'

He still said nothing.

'Bill?'

He got his lower jaw back up. 'You look . . . beautiful.'

Mary blushed demurely. 'Thank you.'

He suddenly remembered his manners. 'Drink?'

She didn't want anything that would distort her senses, not tonight of all nights, even though she felt like drinking a whole bottle of the college port.

'I'll have a soda on its own. There's a siphon over there.'

As he went to oblige, the record finished, the scratching hiss of the needle repeating itself with a regular click. She lifted the arm on to the rest, turned the record over and gently lowered the needle back — just as a yell came from the corner.

Mary turned, saw that he'd managed to soak himself with the siphon.

Chiding, she shook her head in mock despair. 'Honestly — and you fly an aeroplane? Here, take it off and give it to me.'

She went into the kitchen and got a dry tea-towel. Dejectedly Bill stood with his jacket in his hand. 'Sorry — it just shot out.'

Mary took it, then saw that his shirt had a large dark patch down the front. She put the jacket over a chair. 'Undo your top buttons.'

He did as he was told, then she reached in with one hand and held the material as she vigorously rubbed the damp area with the towel.

Bill was conscious of the touch of her fingers on his skin, of her perfume, of her body quivering with the effort. An unstoppable urge exploded in him.

His hands seized her around the waist, as his mouth closed around her sweet-smelling neck.

Mary gasped, responded immediately, abandoning the tea-towel and thrusting her hands on to his bare chest. Buttons flew everywhere.

Somehow they found themselves on the floor, struggling like mad people at their clothing. Mary helped him abandon his shirt, clawing feverishly at his bare back as his hand traversed the length of her leg, pushing up her skirt until he reached her knickers. When he pulled at them they snagged on a suspender. Impatiently she pushed his hand aside and tore them down, the threepenny bit she'd used as a stud spinning away across the floor. Kicking wildly with her feet scuffing the floor, she got them off one leg, leaving them to fly around on her other ankle.

Mary cried out in fleeting pain as Bill's clumsy efforts suddenly resulted in their union.

Afterwards they lay side by side, she snuggled up in his arms.

Bill raised his head and surveyed the scene of abandonment, then let it drop back to stare at the ceiling.

In utter embarrassment he groaned. 'God — I'm so sorry.'

She whispered, hardly daring to trust her voice, 'It was wonderful.'

*Moonlight Serenade,* the record of which they had barely heard the opening bars, had come to an end, the record was scratching away again and again, many times a minute; minute after minute. Unmoving, they lay before the fire hanging on to each other, as if afraid of ever physically parting again.

They ate by candlelight, and later danced, holding each other closely as a man's soft tenor voice came from the wireless.

*'At last my love has come along, my lonely days are over. . . .'*

Mary had abandoned her crumpled dress and was in her black petticoat, Bill only in his shorts and dog-tags.

And then it happened again, only this time they tenderly, unhurriedly, explored each other's bodies, the glowing skin of their youth enhanced by the slumbering redness of the fire.

That night, in the bed where she had first thought she would become a 'real' woman, she lay beside him in the dark, only the faint patch of light coming from the star-dusted heavens showing in the tiny window, and the red glow of his cigarette.

She kissed his naked chest. 'I feel a happily married woman already.'

He played with her hair, his voice imploring, 'You really will marry me, won't you, Mary?'

She poked gently with her finger. 'You try stopping me.'

The music coming from the Bakelite radio they'd found on the floor beneath the bed died away, and the booming stately chimes of Big Ben rang out. The announcer's voice followed the last fading sound of the deep bell. 'This is the nine o'clock news, read by

Alvar Liddell.

Today, large formations of British and American bombers, escorted by fighters, have carried out raids in support of the Allied armies pushing up through Northern France and Belgium. They attacked. . . .'

Hurriedly Mary rolled away from him, reached down and turned it off.

She wanted nothing of the outside to intrude into their little world, their *peaceful* world.

Out there was a terrible war, a great uncertainty; of life and death in the balance for so many. Inside the cosy little cottage with Bill there was certainty, and life . . . and love.

She went to sleep curled into his shape, feeling his warm breath on her neck.

# CHAPTER SIX

Every time it was different. When they awoke, warm and entwined already in each other's arms, it came so naturally that she thought for a moment that she was still dreaming.

Breakfast was special. She fried slices of Spam with eggs they'd bought from a farmer on the way there — miraculously, they'd survived her crash.

Bill helped do the dishes.

When they were finished, and she was spreading the tea-towel so that it would dry, she said: 'Bill — would you mind if we went to church today? There is a beautiful old one in the village.'

He raised an eyebrow quizzically. 'If you want to — sure, but you're not feeling guilty are you? I'd hate to think —'

She cut him off with a wave of the hand. 'No — don't be silly. It's just, well, I love old churches, and the tradition. I'm not a great churchgoer — but I do get a feeling of peace, of timelessness. Oh.' She had a sudden thought. 'I'm not troubling you, am I — I mean I don't know what persuasion you are?'

Bill grinned sheepishly. 'Not at all. I guess before the war I was agnostic — at college anyway — but you don't find many of them in the trenches, as they say.'

Relieved, she brightened. 'Good.'

She waved at the window. Outside it was sunny with a clear sky, a light frost fast disappearing.

'I thought we could have a picnic afterwards.'

Bill nodded, 'OK. I knew you were mad the moment I set eyes on you.'

She gave him a peck on the cheek and skipped away before he could do anything. 'Didn't stop you having your evil way with me though — did it?'

An hour later they were ready. She packed the saddle-bags as he closed the door, found his clips and applied them to his trouser legs.

Happily they cycled away. A couple of miles down the road they started to pass a few houses. Dogs ran out barking and running alongside. Bill kicked out his leg at one. When they went around a bend they were confronted by the church. To Bill it was like a picture off a chocolate box. There was a village green, and beyond it a Norman tower rising above a cedar-tree; beneath the tree was a graveyard of old weathered stones, some leaning at angles, overgrown and neglected.

They parked their bikes just inside the lichgate and entered St Gregory the Great through the doorway, collecting a hymn-book from the old man standing inside.

The church was half-full. When they found a pew and had settled in, Bill looked around at the congregation. They were mostly women, with a sprinkling of old men. There was a lot of coughing in the cold, musty atmosphere. Eventually the organ heralded the arrival of the choir and vicar. The first hymn was announced. The congregation stood to sing 'All things bright and beautiful, all creatures great and small.'

Mary glanced at him; his voice was hesitant and slightly flat. When it came to an end they sat down. The vicar, bald head surrounded by white fluffy hair wheezed as he climbed into the pulpit, and spent an immeasurable time fussing about with his Bible and spectacles.

Eventually he looked around at them all, until his eyes fell on Bill in his uniform.

'It is a pleasure to welcome an officer of the American forces to our little church this morning — a man far from home, far from his family and loved ones, fighting to rid the world of a terrible evil. Please God, it will not be much longer before he can return to the bosom of his family. And that brings us to today's first lesson.'

Out of the corner of her eye she could see that he had gone bright red.

An hour later they emerged into winter sunshine. He murmured into her ear as they waited to thank the vicar: 'I'll get you for this.'

She smiled. 'It wasn't my fault.'

The vicar beamed when it was their turn, and spoke looking only at Mary.

'Good morning to you both, and you my dear, I don't think we've met before, have we?'

Mary was quite forthcoming. 'No, we're just spending a couple of days in the area — our honeymoon actually.'

Mockingly she clung to Bill's arm and looked up adoringly at him. 'Aren't we, dear.'

Bill smiled, though he kept his teeth firmly clamped together. What the hell was she up to now?

The vicar was thrilled, though the three

women with him seemed less so.

'That's wonderful. You must come to the vicarage — we can arrange two extra for lunch, can't we my dear?'

His stern wife looked less than happy at the thought. 'Of course we can.' She took a suddenly horrified Mary by the arm 'Mrs . . . ?'

Desperate, Bill straightened up, intervened. 'First Lieutenant Anderson, ma'am, United States Army Air Force. I'm sorry to say I've got to report back to my squadron — right away.'

The vicar's wife looked triumphant, as did the other ladies.

'Oh what a shame, *Mrs* Anderson.'

They were wished long life and happiness and eventually managed to get to their bicycles. Smiling and waving to parishioners, some of whom even clapped, they set off. When they were out of sight Bill said: 'What the hell got into you?'

'I could see what they were thinking — the women.'

Puzzled, Bill said: 'What?'

Her legs raced around the pedals, making her skirt fly in the wind, setting a pace to carry them away as quickly as possible.

'They kept looking to see if I had a ring on my finger.'

'Oh.'

Bill looked at her hands gripping the handlebars. For the first time he noticed that she was wearing white cotton gloves. She looked across at him and grinned.

'They wanted to get my gloves off. At lunch.'

They found a barn full of hay.

Mary spread a blanket out and unpacked the picnic. With their backs against the wall of hay they dined on Spam sandwiches, some fruit and a little bit of cheese — actually her ration for the whole month.

From the tartan-decorated thermos she poured coffee in the screw-on cup and gave it to him.

He tried to make her go first but she wouldn't have it. 'After your central role this morning, my husband, you deserve it.'

He grinned. 'I ought to put you over my knee.'

Mary giggled, but the thought made her newly awakened sexuality stir.

Bill felt a warmth and contentment the like of which he hadn't had in what seemed a lifetime.

As he dozed off Mary looked at him, full of love — and pain. This time next week . . . She got up, went to the barn entrance, looked back at his still sleeping figure — he looked so boyish. Tears began to well up in her eyes at the thought of the future. Mary could bear it no longer and, pulling her cardigan more tightly around her, went for a walk around the field, crying like a baby.

That evening they stood on the terrace, drinks in one hand, arms around each other's waists.

The sky was ablaze with stars that sparkled in the cold air like millions of diamonds spilled on black velvet, with the Milky Way a slash of brilliance directly above their heads.

Mary murmured: 'Isn't it marvellous?'

Bill kissed the top of her head.

'I've never noticed before.'

She turned to him, smiled suggestively.

'Maybe our senses are different now?'

He chuckled knowingly, took her drink and put it on the table with his.

'Here.'

He took her hand and to her surprise sat down on the cold stone.

'Come on.'

Mary giggled, completely mystified.

'Whatever are you doing?'

He pulled her gently down, then leant back flat out on the ground and put his arm out for her to rest her head on.

Mystified, she lay down beside him. Bill pointed upwards as he raised his legs.

'Look, with you I'm walking on the stars.'

'Why — you old romantic.'

But she did the same, seeing the dark shape of her feet against the luminescent sky. Giggling like children they lay there, pretending to walk the heavens. Eventually she looked across at him, at this man who had literally and metaphorically turned her world upside down.

'It's wonderful — like flying in space, with the stars *beneath* us.'

Tired of their game they stayed still for sometime in silence gazing up at the heavens, sensing a moment that they knew they would remember for as long as they lived.

Later, in front of the fire, they bathed in a galvanized metal bathtub he'd found on the outside wall of the scullery.

Mary went first, sitting up in it, the firelight flickering on her nakedness. She'd tied her hair up. Bill gently, lovingly soaped her back and shoulders.

Finally, wrapped in dressing-gowns belonging to the cottage, they sat on the floor, Bill with his back to the sofa, she leaning against him. Only the wavering light of the fire and a candle by the wireless lit the room.

A BBC announcer said: 'So, from the Corn Exchange, Bedford, the BBC Symphony Orchestra will perform Beethoven's Fifth Symphony.'

Applause died away, and the music, after a pause, made its dramatic opening statement, the theme of which, repeated on a muted drum and broadcast nightly to all the occupied countries of Europe, brought hope when all else had died.

On their last night in the little bedroom he'd gone to sleep at last, curled like a little boy — a child — at her breast.

Again she wondered at the diversity of the act of love; something her sheltered existence had never entertained. Earlier, when they'd slid into the cold bed, she first, it had just happened. It had started as horseplay, tickling and smacking, and ended with her face down, held firmly but gently by his hand on her neck. He made love to her without her once seeing him, her eyes heavy-lidded as with a grunt she was moved forward by the force of their union.

And now? She kissed the top of his head and gently stroked the curls from his face.

From master to helpless boy; something a woman obviously had to get used to. She smiled into the darkness, secure in the knowledge that Bill was the gentlest of men, that they would be equals in all they did.

She came to the station to see him off. They were wrapped in each other's arms, loath to let go, to be physically parted. She didn't cry, she'd done that the day before, would do it again, many times, but not now: she'd resolved not to let him see the tears.

Bill was going to get permission from his CO to get married. They wanted it as soon as possible. She'd got his address, he hers. Both were writing that night — and every night.

A wisp of smoke in the distance announced the arrival of a train, for once on time. The locomotive clanked past, all hissing steam, the driver leaning out of his cab, flashing her a glance as he passed by.

When the carriages had squealed to a halt there was a corridor door right beside them. He opened it, threw in his bag, and then took her in his arms again, holding her tight, his cheek hard against hers. Mary fought back the tears. At last Bill let go, kissed her, then climbed into the coach, tugging the leather strap and dropping the window before slamming the door and leaning out. They kissed again, then with his hands still cupping her face she said: 'I love you Bill. I love you so much.'

He looked into her eyes. 'I know, and I love you even more.'

A lump was already forming in her throat. She looked anxiously down the length of the train, frightened of seeing the guard with his green flag — the seconds were running out.

Bill said: 'I'm going to try and get an overnight pass — as soon as the weather boys say we can't go. Can I call the college number you gave me — will you get the message?'

Mary, now losing her struggle to hold back her tears, nodded. 'Of course — and don't forget the number of my other digs when I'm on my war work. And I could come to you if you like — even if it's only for a couple of hours.'

'Great, we'll work something out, don't you worry.'

And then Mary's fear became reality as the guard waved the green flag and blew long and hard on his whistle.

There was an answering call from the locomotive. They were in each other's arms again, Bill almost half-out of the window.

'Excuse me, Lieutenant.'

Another American grabbed the door handle and began to open it. Bill had to part from her as the man boarded and the door slammed shut.

He ducked out, and grabbed her again. But now the train was on the move.

Mary trotted, still holding his hand.

'You won't leave me, Bill, will you — ever?'

'No. We'll be together now — *always.*'

They had to let go as a station column and a couple of milk churns got in the way, and the speed of the train steadily increased.

At last she could no longer keep up, her progress being impeded by knots of waving people, mostly women.

As he drew further away she called: 'Take care.'

He continued waving as the coaches lurched around points and curves, until he was lost from sight.

Mary turned and walked back, giving up her platform ticket and stepping out into the forecourt. Utterly bereft, she made her way into the city. She felt so lonely — something she had never before experienced, she had always been happy in her own company. But now, it was as if a part of her had been torn away.

# CHAPTER SEVEN

Bill got back to the squadron after dark. Even before he dumped his bag in his room he went straight to the adjutant's office in one of the Quonset huts clustered all around the field.

A corporal stood up when he entered.

'Is the adjutant in?'

'No sir. He's gone into Ipswich with the CO — some sort of civic reception. They won't be back till quite late, sir.'

Disappointed, Bill frowned. 'I guess it can wait till morning.'

The corporal hesitated. 'I don't think he'll have time, Lieutenant. There is a big flap on tomorrow — max effort — and you're on the list.'

He picked up a sheet of typed paper and held it out. Bill took it, noted his name and handed it back.

'Grapevine say where we're going?'

'No sir. Nothing down from Group yet.'

Frustrated, Bill returned the non-com's salute. Outside there was rain in the wind. He wondered what the Met report was. He shared his room in an old RAF wooden hut that had seen better days. As soon as he stepped into the narrow corridor he could smell the damp.

Kelleher was stretched out on his bunk, reading a cheap paperback with a lurid cover.

'Hi there. Have a good time?'

Bill chucked his bag on to his bed. 'Yep.'

'What did you do? Any chicks?'

Bill didn't want to talk about Mary, especially to Kelleher. He said something non-committal.

After the train journey he felt dirty and took a quick shower, letting the hot water pour on to the top of his head, keeping his eyes closed. He wondered what she was doing right then.

At the officers' club he was greeted by the crowd. He told no one about Mary — he wanted to see the adjutant first. The gossip was that they might be moved to mainland Europe to give tactical support to the armies very soon.

Apparently the black-and-white recognition stripes of the tactical air force were already being painted on the wings and fuselages of some of the planes.

Moodily he munched on his supper, a beefburger and fries, and sipped a coke. People drifted away, getting an early night.

He finished his cigarette and then went to see his crew chief, checking that his ship had completed the overhaul that had been promised.

That night he stretched out in bed, imagining Mary was with him, holding one of her silk scarves with her perfume in his hand.

When he eventually drifted off to sleep it was quite late.

She spent the afternoon in the college library, staring unseen into the winter's gloom. She kept imagining that first meeting, Bill standing near the books, the sun falling in dusty rays through the window on to his face.

Mentally she had to keep pinching herself that it had happened — though her body occasionally told her it was no dream.

She tore a sheet of paper from one of the pads supplied by the War Office for her work, and began her first letter to a man whom she loved dearly, more than life itself, and who she knew loved her. Yet only a week encompassed their entire knowledge of the existence of each other. Unbelievable.

Tomorrow and the next few days she was at Bletchley Park. There, amongst the quiet but intense activity — at least in her hut — she guessed that some form of normality would return. And the communications she was being asked to assess for their vernacular meaning were becoming increasingly horrendous — things were happening all over eastern Europe in camps, not for prisoners of war, but civilians. They had known of them for some time, but now increased rail activity into them was being monitored.

She finished her first letter, apologized for its being so brief, but others, she swore, would be longer.

That evening she packed the few things she needed to take with her to her digs in Bletchley. Her train tomorrow, going via Bedford, was an early one.

When she eventually got into her bed it seemed so lonely — so cold. A big sob suddenly came from nowhere.


A hand shook him by the shoulder. Bill groaned, tried to free himself, kept his eyes closed.

The hand shook him again, roughly.

'Sir, time to rise and shine.'

He slept on. It happened again, this time the shaking continued until his eyes opened.

He growled, 'All right, Melanic, put a sock in it.'

He pushed himself up into a sitting position, then swung his feet to the floor, holding his sleep-befuddled head in his hands, dog tags swinging like pendulums.

'You really awake, sir?'

'For Christ's sake, Melanic, I'm not sleepwalking.'

Melanic shoved a cup of hot sweet coffee on the floor before him, between his bare legs.

'Breakfast starts in half an hour, sir.'

Bill grunted and took the mug. His dog tags clinked against the china and dropped into the coffee. He snatched them out, hot drips of liquid splashing his bare chest.

'Oh crap.'

But it helped to wake him up. He padded to the john in his shorts, then pulled them off and took a towel to the shower block.

Half a dozen men were already occupying the steaming row. The water was at first bitterly cold when he pulled the chain, but soon it was streaming down over his head and body, making him tingle with heat.

Showered, shaved and dressed in flying coveralls and his leather jacket, he grabbed his cap and stepped outside. He took his first lungful of fresh air. For the next few hours he would be flying at altitude on oxygen, mouth parched and lips cracking from the dry gas.

So he looked upon this moment as his morning drink of the sea-moist, air of England.

Bill joined the throng eating early-morning breakfast of powdered eggs — they gave you less gas at altitude. The briefing took place in the squadron dispersal hut. The CO with officers from wing and group were present.

Bill found that they were going to provide the bomber force with top cover over the target and for the withdrawal; the target being Berlin, as it had been with increasing frequency since D Day. German fighters often waited for the great bomber armadas to turn for home, when their fighter escorts would be low on fuel, before attacking.

So their group would use drop-tanks for extra gas and arrive over Berlin ready to relieve the fighters who had done the insertion cover. The CO wished them all good luck and good hunting, then left with the briefing officers. There was no way Bill could say anything to him, and in any case there were proper channels to go through. It was two hours before take-off. He went to the squadron office, where he struck lucky.

The adjutant, an elderly major in his forties, saw him immediately. He rose from behind his desk as Bill saluted. He acknowledged, then held his hand out.

'Get a good leave?'

The corporal who had followed Bill into the room put some papers before the adjutant, who picked up his pen, indicating for Bill to sit down.

'Excuse me a moment.'

The pen scratched as the papers were scanned and signed, then picked up one at a time by the corporal. When the signing was finished, the NCO left, closing the door behind him.

'Now, what can I do for you?'

Bill ran his hand nervously through his hair. 'I want to get married — an English girl in Cambridge. I've come for the boss's approval.'

'Hm — I see. Is she pregnant?'

The question shocked Bill who snapped, 'No. Certainly not.'

The older man shrugged. 'You aren't the first, and by God you won't be the last to come through this office seeking to marry a pregnant popsy.' He caught the flash of anger on Bill's face. 'No offence.'

He leant back in his chair. 'What I'm try-ing to say is, whether you are in love or not — and half the men I get in here haven't really thought it through, the CO will say *No,* believe me.'

Bill felt winded, his shoulders dropped. The adjutant didn't like doing it, in fact he was a kindly man, and tried not to let a man's hope and excitement ride for days before his dreams were shattered. He knew that Bill was due off on a mission, and was worried at the effect that it seemed to have on him.

'I know I shouldn't do this — but I think a medicinal brandy is called for.'

Whilst Bill slumped in his chair the adju-tant got up, unlocked a cupboard and brought out a bottle and two tumblers. He splashed a measure into each glass and handed one to Bill.

'Blame it on the Flight-Surgeon if anyone asks.'

Bill took the glass, held it in both hands. There was a determined edge to his voice.

'I'm going to marry this girl, sir. I want to do it, and *soon* — in case anything happens . . .' Frowning, he downed the brandy in one. The adjutant, sitting on the corner of his desk, slowly swinging his leg which ached abominably in this wet English climate, sipped his sedately.

'Well, I'll pass your application on — give it my best go, I promise, but I tell you now, the Old Man will say *No.*'

Bill looked up at him, lips set in a tight line. 'But why?'

The adjutant took another sip. 'Oh — something to do with the trouble they had after the First World War. Over ninety per cent of dough boys' marriages failed.'

Bill set the glass down on the desk. 'Well, I intend to proceed, sir. Do I need to put it in writing?'

The adjutant nodded. 'I'll get the typing-pool to do it now — you can sign it before you leave. Excuse me.'

He went to his intercom and buzzed. Almost immediately the corporal appeared.

'Yes sir?'

What was wanted was explained. 'Do it straight away.' The adjutant checked his watch. 'The lieutenant here is flying on this morning's mission — he will sign it before he leaves.'

'Yes, sir.'

They were alone again.

The adjutant put the bottle back, rinsed out the glasses in a little corner sink and dried them, eyeing up Bill.

'Special, is she?'

Bill nodded. 'I know you must have heard it all before, but, this is genuine. Both of us — well — hit it off. But that sounds too casual, too light. We're made for each other.'

He chewed his lip. 'I'm not a fool, sir — this war is not over yet — a lot of people aren't going to make it through to the end — and then there's Japan. I want to be married to her — her name's Mary by the way, more than anything else in the world. I want her to have my name — in case anything . . . That's why it's so important — so urgent.' His voice tailed away in embarrassment.

Before the adjutant could murmur something calming, reassuring, Bill suddenly looked up sharply. 'What if I do it without the Old Man's permission?'

The older man shook his head firmly. 'Don't even think of it, Bill. They might court-martial you, or ship you straight back home or to the Far East in disgrace — it would ruin your record after the war, close down a lot of career opportunities.'

Bill shrugged his indifference. Worried, the adjutant pressed on. 'You wouldn't see your young lady for years — maybe never again.'

There was a knock on the door. The adjutant opened it and spoke to someone outside. When he turned back to Bill the latter looked angrily back up at him. 'I can't see how anyone has the right —'

Frustrated with his lack of progress the adjutant chopped his open palm with the edge of his other hand. 'You're in the army, son. They have *every* right.'

Corporal Johnson knocked and entered, setting a typewritten sheet down on the desk. 'There we are, sir.'

Bill stood up, scanned the simple request and signed it. He faced the adjutant.

'I'm grateful for all your help.' It was said without rancour.

'That's OK — I understand your feelings, believe me.'

'When will I know, sir?'

The adjutant returned to his seat, steepled his hands and brought the tips of his fingers to his pursed lips. 'He's very busy — we've got quite a lot going on — but I'll try and get an answer from him by — say six p.m.? He's on today's show as you know, despite this proposed move we're working on.'

Bill saluted. 'I'm obliged.'

The adjutant looked out of the window as Bill hurried away, feeling sorry for the guy. He felt for the young men to whom he had to be a sort of father figure, and for the fact that so many would never be going home again — not even in a body bag. That damned expression: *'no known grave'* haunted him. The weather was good: killing weather.

Outside the sound of Merlin-Packard engines being kicked into life and run up concentrated Bill's mind on the matter in hand. In the crew room he put on his flying-boots, slipped his Mae West over his leather jacket, picked up his helmet, oxygen mask and parachute and joined a bunch who were catching a ride on a six by six truck to the hardstands. Joking and punching and pulling at each other they exchanged farewells. 'See you soon.' 'On a wing and a prayer' came a rejoinder.

His crew chief was waiting and helped him into the cockpit, securing his oxygen and radio lines and tightening the webbing of the safety harness.

The familiar smell of oil, rubber, and gas assailed his nostrils.

He gave a thumbs up, and the 1,590 horse power of the Merlin-Packard coughed and snorted into life.

Immediately the whole ship became a living shuddering entity. The chocks were pulled away.

Bill gave a salute to the crew chief and eased the throttle forward. He joined the

145

line making their way around the peritrack, their propwash blowing the grass flat. The waves rippled away across the field, the boundary fence bushes waved wildly like a crowd saying goodbye: the dawn chorus of 1944. The birds of war were waking.

At the runway, the CO took off first, with his wingman in formation, the others following.

When it came to his turn, Bill watched the two before him begin their roll, then eased forward and lined up into the wind, gave a quick three-count and with a thumbs-up to his wingman, gave it the gas.

Breaking ground he pulled up the gear and started milking up the flaps, catching up with those before him within a mile of the strip.

They settled into tactical combat formation and linked up with other squadrons in the group, all the time climbing. At 5,000 feet Bill suddenly remembered to do his visual post-take-off check of the cockpit which he had, unusually, forgotten.

Everything was OK, but he felt on edge. Had he been subconsciously thinking about Mary, so that things he did routinely were not kicking in? It was sloppy, and there was no room for that in this business.

The weather was perfect, visibility unlimited. Long before they crossed the Dutch coast he could see the Rhine, curving back and forth on itself like a silver serpent, until it was lost in a far-distant haze.

It didn't seem possible that there were Germans down there, or that away to the right the Allied Armies were engaged in a fierce battle.

It all looked so peaceful.

Mary showed her pass and walked up the main drive at Bletchley Park, before turning off to her hut situated at the back. On the way over, on the train, she had started on another letter to Bill.

It had soon dawned on her that she couldn't fill it up all the time with protestations of love, that she had to include other things. Unfortunately she was unable to tell him about her war work, and frankly the university stuff was dull to anybody outside the field. She day-dreamed once again of their time together. In Bill she had found her kindred spirit, like Emily Brontë's Cathy had done in *Wuthering Heights,* and with it came the realization that her existence now had real meaning.

As if in answer to her prayers for something to write about, she had been delayed at Bedford. A V1 flying bomb had dropped on the signalling system somewhere. They were told there would be an hour's delay, so she had wandered towards the town centre.

Mary reached a river bridge and leant on the stone balustrade, gazing down at the wide river which curved gently away to a beautiful arched Victorian footbridge.

The river-bank was lined with public gardens and large trees. On one side was a bijou little cinema, and next door a boating yard with punts moored in rows outside. On the other side an old Georgian Inn: the Swan. It was all so beautiful — so England.

The road was quiet except for the odd van and doctor's car, and the occasional convoy of trucks servicing the many airfields in the district.

On the town side of the bridge there was a square in which stood a church with a tall spire, and the Corn Exchange, from where the broadcast of Beethoven's Fifth had come. She noticed a poster proclaiming that Dame Myra Hess was giving one of her recitals that she had made so famous at the National Gallery.

The High Street was, as in Cambridge, full of aimlessly wandering servicemen. Eventually she got a cup of tea and bun at the Lyons teashop.

She nearly missed her train — would have

had it not been for a delay caused by crowds of soldiers at the WVS caravan in the St John's station yard where mugs of tea were being served.

Mary entered her hut. Her supervisor, an old civil servant who had been knighted in 1935, looked up at her from above his half-moon spectacles.

'Good afternoon, Doctor, so glad you could join us.'

Despite the sarcasm, he was an old dear really, and looked after 'his girls' with vigour, so much so that he had endeared himself to them all as — behind his back of course — *'Pa-pa.'*

'I'm sorry, Sir George, there was a doodle-bug — did something to the signalling.'

He sniffed. 'We've got a lot on, and it's nasty.'

Mary took the file he handed her, eager to play her part in the victory over the forces that had once threatened to end a way of life that had taken a 1,000 years to evolve: the same length of time as the Third Reich was supposed to last.

When they crossed the coast the flak suddenly appeared, the deadly black puffs of smoke sliding by underneath. Bill observed

149

one of the planes from the formation below peeling off for home, losing altitude and smoking a little.

Everyone spread out now, weaving and dipping their wings, searching the skies above, below, in front and behind. He was doing a lot of rubbernecking — it was the best way there was of staying alive.

They still had their long-range fuel tanks, so when the leader's voice came over the R/T, ordering them to drop them, it was like a big load rolling off his back.

The flak died away and they flew on in peace. Still being vigilant, he occasionally thought of Mary, feeling somehow that she was with him. It gave him comfort.

Over half an hour later a huge bank of haze appeared up ahead, with hundreds of white contrails leading into it, alerting them to the fact that Berlin was near. Seconds later they saw the vast bomber fleets ahead and below.

It gave him a lift to see so many planes, some olive-green, others bright silver. The great battle formation was exhilarating, invincible-looking. But he knew better.

Flak started murderously to assault the B17s and Liberators; he could see the bursts, hundreds of them, sprouting all around. Such was his height that to Bill it looked as though the massed formations were standing still, while the black puffs were floating through them on an invisible stream. It was a phenomenon of high-altitude flying that never failed to fascinate him.

There was a sudden flash down in the lead box, and where there had once been a Liberator — and its crew — there was just a bigger mass of smoke drifting back. The others didn't waiver, just ploughed steadily on towards the target. Bill admired the courage, knew he couldn't do it.

The group's timing was, for once, perfect. On the outskirts of Berlin they took over from the penetration squadrons, as was supposed to happen.

As the bombers started their final run to the target, Bill and his wing were weaving above them. They were just drawing ahead when he saw green flares coming up from the lead Fortresses, requesting help as twenty to thirty Messerschmitt 109s prepared for a head-on attack.

The low squadron turned in to cut them off, as over the R/T a young voice yelled in panic: 'Above — Jesus — above.' Bill snatched his head up, saw FW 190s barreling down on them, the leading edges of their wings winking and flashing as they fired

151

their cannons.

He rammed the throttle against the stop and held it there as they turned to meet them.

Several of the first 190s had too much speed for them to be intercepted, and they swept past. The next were caught in one big dogfight.

Somehow he found himself on the tail of one. He got off a deflection burst and watched the Focke-Wulf turn into his line of fire.

There were flashes and something came tumbling past that made him duck and yell out with fright. The 190 flipped over and fell away like a flaming meteor to earth.

Bill swung back — to be confronted by a head-on view of the bombers.

Screaming in terror, he slid under the huge shape of the first Fortress.

Then ship after ship, section after section, some with bombs spilling out of their open doors, flashed past. Finally, miraculously, he was clear.

Soaked in sweat, he thumbed his radio-transmitter. 'Blue leader here, anyone around?'

The response seemed right beside him, made his over-tense body jump.

'Yeah, I'm behind you.'

He slewed his ship and saw him.

Unbelievably his wingman had followed him through the entire episode. Both of them had come out without a scratch.

They caught up with the bomber stream, following the contrails and climbing up through them just as three more 190s flew head-on into the formation. At the last moment the enemy rolled on to their backs and, still firing, flashed down through the bombers. The last one left it a split second too late. He started to roll away, but the Fortress was already on him. His wing hit the bomber in number three engine. The tangled blazing mass went tumbling down through the formation. Bill felt sick at what could so easily have been his fate.

His wingman spotted a straggler, a lone Liberator with smoke pouring from one engine. It was falling behind and losing altitude and the Krauts were buzzing around him like flies. He was dishing it out as well, all turrets twinkling and tracer flying out at the 109s.

But by the time they got there it was too late to do much.

The bomber had started into a shallow dive and two white 'chutes had blossomed out, but the tail-gunner was still in there fighting.

The tracer kept on coming until the Liberator spun into woods. There was a flash, and a tall column of black smoke.

Bill closed with one of the circling Messerschmitts, whose pilot seemed not to have noticed them: he was probably a rookie barely out of training. The Germans were getting desperate. Bill was so near when he opened fire that the 109 just blew apart, its wings whirling away in a grotesque flight of their own. His radio exploded in his ears.

'Break left, break left.'

Bill yanked the stick over, his vision dimming with the G force.

Suddenly there was a 'thump' as if the plane had been kicked by a giant, and the smell of cordite filled the cockpit.

The 109 was so close behind he could see a large yellow spinner and flashes from the cannons in its nose. Almost immediately the wingman's exultant shout rang in his earphones. 'I got him.'

The grey fuselage with its cross was suddenly covered in flames. It flicked over and dived down, going into a field on its back, leaving a trail of burning fuel along the ground.

Bill, soaked with sweat and urine heard himself thanking his wingman as if it was somebody else speaking. He was shaking like a leaf, glad that he couldn't be seen. He jerked his head in all directions.

The sky was empty.

Bill checked his fuel and Ts & Ps. He was worried about the hit, but all seemed in order.

'Come on, time to go home.'

# Chapter Eight

That evening Mary went with two other girls to the pictures, queuing for ten minutes to get in.

They sat through a good 'B' film. When the lights came up for the interval, a crowd of young soldiers started flirting with them. The others played along, but Mary was just polite.

She just couldn't stop thinking about Bill: where was he, what was he doing, above all — was he safe?

She had found relief at work, where the atmosphere was always intense, sometimes exhilarating, sometimes soul-destroying, always involving, though the work in different huts was never spoken about. But everyone knew it was very special.

But, once away, she'd felt miserable, so when a couple of the girls from another hut who shared her digs said they were going to the flicks she'd readily agreed.

The lights dimmed, a spotlight shone down, and out of the bowels of the orchestra-pit an organ rose; the organist, dressed in a dinner jacket, beamed and bounced on his stool as he played a vigorous fast number.

For the next ten minutes they were treated to tunes from the shows — *The Desert Song, The Girl Friend* and others, and ending with the popular theme of the night's feature film. Then the organ started to descend, still being played, the man still beaming and acknowledging the applause.

The spotlight shrank until only his grinning face with his glasses reflecting the light showed, with the last notes, it was extinguished and there was blackness.

The house lights came back up and the soldiers started talking to them again. One of her friends whispered in her ear: 'I think I might be finding my own way home. Why don't you join in, Mary? That young man there is very nice — he's educated, you know. Something to do with radar — whatever that is.'

Should she tell them about Bill? Mary was a very private person. She was worried about what they would say, what anyone would say, and the thought of the teasing she would get — the remarks of 'You a

Yankee Basher' was too appalling to seriously consider saying anything. Only her parents need know. She frowned. That wouldn't be easy — not as regarded her father.

Mercifully, further thought was cut off as simultaneously the house lights dimmed and with a click the curtains started to open; the projector was already showing the crowing cockerel of the Pathé News on the still rippling-material, accompanied by stirring music and rousing commentary. Pictures of the Queen visiting soldiers injured in battle since D Day followed, then an item about a dog show.

After the news came the trailer for next week. There was a rustle of anticipation when it ended, and the house lights stayed down. It was time for the big feature.

*Love Story* filled the screen, starring Margaret Lockwood, Stewart Granger, and her favourite: Patricia Roc. The popular theme music, *Cornish Rhapsody* swelled from the soundtrack — violins and woodwind, and a piano — not like the organ.

As soon as he'd finished debriefing Bill took a shower. Then, dressed in fresh kit, he made his way to see the adjutant.

When he came out of his hut it was dusk

and bitterly cold, the wind coming across the airfield from the northeast. He pulled his collar up and held it with his fist, under his chin.

The squadron office was in darkness. Cursing, he stumbled over a bicycle in the gloom.

Once inside, with the blackout curtain redrawn, he released his collar and pulled it down.

The sergeant behind a desk stood up and saluted.

'How may I help you, sir?'

Bill returned the salute.

'My name is Anderson. I wish to see the adjutant, he'll be expecting me.'

Something in the sergeant's look when he heard his name made his heart sink.

'Yes, sir. Just a moment.'

He tapped at the door behind him and put his head around the edge.

'Lieutenant Anderson to see you, sir.'

Bill didn't hear any reply, but the sergeant pushed the door further open and stood aside.

'Please go in, sir.'

The adjutant's face confirmed his suspicions.

Without saying anything the major fished a sheet of typewritten paper out of a folder, and with two fingers pushed it across the desk at him, turning it around as he did so.

Only then did he speak.

'I'm sorry, Bill, the Old Man has turned down your application. Request for permission to marry — denied.'

To Bill, it felt as if a cold hand had suddenly squeezed his heart.

He looked up. 'I have to see the CO. I *must* see him.'

The adjutant shook his head.

'Pointless, and in any case impossible. In the next couple of weeks this squadron is being transferred to France, we're joining Nineteenth Tactical Air Command to support the troops. The CO has already left — there is a lot to sort out.'

His world fell apart. Not only was he not being allowed to marry Mary, but he wouldn't even be able to see her regularly — might never see her again.

Whether it was the exhaustion of the day or what, but he almost did a bunk, back to Mary, perhaps to the cottage, maybe somewhere else. But being AWOL? It would only be a matter of time before the MPs came a-knocking. And where would that leave Mary? Humiliated.

Devastated, he wandered out into the night. He had no conscious thought of what to do next, but the severity of the cold drove him to the officers club. Mechanically he ordered a beer. He hadn't touched it when a guy climbed on to a stool beside him.

'You OK, Bill, you look pretty beat?'

He grunted, eventually managed: 'They've refused me permission to marry.'

'Who has?'

He explained what had happened.

The other first lieutenant frowned. 'I should check it out. Go and see somebody in the judge advocate's office at Wing HQ.'

Bill looked at him, hardly daring to have his hopes raised. 'On what grounds?'

The man spread his hands on the bar top. 'Hell, I'm no lawyer, but I heard of a guy at Kimbolton who had similar trouble, and he ended up marrying.' He shook his head sadly. 'Unfortunately he bought the farm the day after he came back from his honeymoon.'

'You say at Wing HQ?'

'Yes. Hey, aren't you going to finish your beer?'

But Bill was already outside the hut that housed the club and grabbing one of the many base bikes from its concrete slot. Despite the gloom he pedalled like hell in the direction of Wing, dark shapes yelling at him as he brushed past, then he was out of the main gate, wobbling around the barrier, down the road to some brick buildings on the outskirts of a village.

He threw away the machine and entered the main door, throwing a quick salute to a startled major who was just leaving.

A snowdrop and a corporal were talking by the reception desk. Both looked up in surprise as he burst in.

He returned their salutes.

'The judge advocate's office — is anybody there? It's important.'

'Just a moment, sir.'

The corporal plugged in a lead on the switchboard.

Waiting, Bill could hardly contain himself. Eventually the connection must have been made as the corporal spoke into his handset. 'Desk here, is there anyone who can see. . . .'

He looked up. 'Sorry Sir — your name?'

Bill told him.

'. . . a First Lieutenant Anderson, sir.'

There was a pause as the corporal listened, then he turned to Bill. 'Major Jenner has left, sir, there is only a Lieutenant Riley. He's new, came in from Stateside less than forty-eight hours ago, says he may not be able to help you if it's anything to do with English civil law.'

'It's not, and I must see him.'

The corporal spoke briefly into the telephone, then replaced the receiver.

'The lieutenant says go right on in, sir — room eleven.'

He strode down the corridor, checking the numbers, feeling almost light-headed. He gave number eleven a perfunctory knock and entered.

The man had his back to him, leaning forward, hands on a desk. When he turned, Bill saw that he had been studying a large textbook. He was bright-eyed behind his rimless glasses, tall and thin.

They shook hands. 'Good of you to see me,' Bill said. 'I guess you were about to knock off?'

'That's OK, I was just boning up a little on local law. I gather it's busy around here, what with poaching, to say nothing of the ladies and booze. We have a lot of liaison work to do with the courts. Now — what's the problem?'

Bill explained. Riley listened, then held up his hand.

'Your friend is correct — in *theory*. The CO has no right to ban you from marrying anybody — you're an officer, it's different for enlisted men.'

Bill's heart leapt — then he remembered

that the CO was not going to be available for days — maybe a week or two, and somehow, knowing the Old Man, he knew that there would be no changing his mind on the say-so of some junior officer — even from the judge advocate's branch.

Glumly he explained to Riley, showed him the typed answer. The legal officer stroked his chin as he thought, then he said: 'What you need to do, therefore, is petition a higher authority, right up through the chain of command, if necessary to the very top.'

Eagerly Bill said: 'Can we do that? Will *you* do that?'

Riley grinned roguishly. 'You bet. Is she worth it?'

'*Yes.*'

'That's good, because it might be marked on your record, and blight your career prospects in this man's army.'

At that they both laughed.

After four days there was still no letter from Bill. Disappointed, Mary left Bletchley for Cambridge. There was no letter at her lodgings. Unable to rest unless she was absolutely sure, she hurried across a foggy Backs and into the college and the porter's lodge.

The porter, in his maroon waistcoat and striped shirt-sleeves, was coincidentally just giving a letter to somebody.

'Good evening, Doctor Rice. Did you have a good journey?'

She nodded and tried to be as casual as possible. 'Yes, thank you, Sam, and you — how is your wife?'

He grimaced. 'This cold and dampness don't suit her arthritis one bit.'

He grumbled on for a while, until she could wait no longer.

'Any letters for me?'

Dobson turned to his oak pigeon-holes and came back with three. 'There we are, Doctor. Will you be dining in tonight?'

It took all her self-control not to snatch them, and say as casually as possible, 'Yes — yes of course.'

As she hurried away across the foggy courtyard, he shook his head and wondered aloud: 'Who'd have thought that a serious well-bred girl like that would be so obviously besotted — and with a Yank of all people.'

Mary looked down at the letters when she was safely round the corner.

Disappointingly, two were obviously not from him — but the third *was.*

She tore it open, her eyes devouring the words. It was so short.

'Darling Mary,

Have just managed to get this off to you — pretty busy here.

I have started arrangements for permission to marry you. I love you so much. Please take good care of yourself — for *me.* I want to spend the rest of my life with you.

Darling, if I am to get this through the censorship boys and into the post-room tonight I've got to sign off quick. Will write again tomorrow — or maybe the day after.

Love you — love you — love you.

Yours, Bill.'

Mary held it to her lips, kissed it where he had marked his kisses with crosses. Tears were streaming down her face.

Tense, and on the edge of his seat, Bill had been flying in atrocious conditions for hours. A huge fog bank had descended over Northern Europe which rose up from the ground to 20,000 feet. They were supposed to be escorting home a large raid on Augsburg, but now the bombers were scattered all over the place, as were their fighter escorts. The Luftwaffe were fortunately in similar trouble.

They were ordered to turn for home.

Time seemed to pass agonizingly slowly, and his cramped tense frame and sore eyes from watching the instruments was beginning to tell on him. They flew at a few hundred feet over the North Sea, the fog seeming to get even thicker by the minute. When suddenly all forward view disappeared, Bill panicked. Seconds later his fear turned to soaring relief as he came out of the smoke clouds of a convoy that had been the cause of the sudden complete loss of visibility. Ahead he could just make out the coast of England.

Passing inland he recognized the huge emergency landing-strip located between Lowestoft and Leiston. He was sorely tempted to land, but the urge to get back, to get news about his application to Wing was too much.

He set course for base, conscious of others going down to get the hell out of the murderous weather.

When he landed some half an hour later, he was one of only four in the squadron to do so. The rest, and other squadrons, had landed all over the east of England. Miraculously no one was lost, but it was to be two days before they could all be reassembled for further combat duties.

Down on the ground, Bill had to be helped from the cockpit by the crew chief and his number one. As he was unable to stand they massaged his cramped limbs as he lay on the soaking wet grass.

As soon as he could he checked with operations — there would be no flying for at least twenty-four hours, probably longer.

After waiting in turn, he called Mary's college — the porter's lodge — and asked for a message to be delivered to Doctor Rice.

Mary was in the senior common room, sipping a cup of tea beside the fire, when the boy from the porter's office came in with a silver salver.

She looked up as he came towards her, her heart already beating faster even before he said: 'Doctor Rice — telephone message.'

She didn't want to take it. Urgent messages more often than not meant bad news.

But she did.

It took seconds for the message to sink in.

The fog got even thicker at dusk; the train crawled through the deep, dark night, frequently stopping for long intervals. At last, some one and a half hours late it trundled into the dimly lit station and squealed to a halt.

Bill got out, doors slammed. He made his way with a host of dark, dispirited shapes into the damp, freezing booking-hall with its wooden floor and smell of coal-gas.

As he shuffled forward in the crowd for the exit he caught sight of a figure in the corner, sitting on a wooden bench, wrapped in a coat with a high collar.

# CHAPTER NINE

Mary saw him at the same time. She flew into his arms as he dropped his bag, and they hung on to each other, saying nothing as the crowd bumped and stumbled past. Eventually the number of passengers dwindled until they were alone. At last their lips met.

A piercing whistle and a blast of steam heralded the departure of the train on the way north.

She snuggled into his chest as, still wrapped in each other's arms, they left the station, walking into the swirling fog as the sound of the engine, it's smoke exhausting in great chuffs, laboured away unseen into the night. It was so dark it was as if they were the only people in the world.

Mary said: 'Darling, I can't believe it.'

'Neither can I.' He held on to her tightly. 'For once the Met people really fouled up.' He hesitated, then asked: 'There is no way we can get to the cottage, is there?'

He felt her shake her head.

'Impossible.'

'Oh.' His disappointment was obvious.

She squeezed him. 'Don't worry. You can come and stay in my room.'

Bill was shocked. 'You mean — at your digs?'

She chuckled. 'No, you dafty — I couldn't see Mrs Chick allowing that.'

'Where, then?'

She grinned unseen in the dark against his chest, and said mischievously: 'I've got us a room.'

Bill stopped in his tracks.

'Hell, where?'

She kept her face down as she replied: 'A colleague has a flat she's not using. Lucky isn't it?'

She didn't mention the fact that she'd positively bribed the woman to move out for the night, by volunteering to do her next two nights of fire-watching up on the cold roof of the college.

Anyway, the woman darned well knew why she needed it; apparently she had somebody herself.

The flat was nearer the station than the city centre. It was in a converted Edwardian town house.

Mary led the way into the communal hall with its grand staircase, and opened the first door on the right — the old drawing-room. Everywhere was cold and musty.

The front half was now the high-ceilinged sitting-room. A partition made the rear portion into a bedroom and a small kitchenette.

He dropped his bag and looked around. 'Where's the bathroom?'

'Down the hall — behind the stairs.'

He grimaced. 'I need to freshen up.'

Mary opened the kitchenette door, looked at the old-fashioned gas-cooker and the wooden meat-safe. 'Do you want anything to eat?'

Bill paused. 'Hell, I don't want to put you to any bother, just a snack if there is anything. I was on that darned train for hours.'

'Right, I'll see what we've got.'

Mary kept her coat on, bending to light the gas-fire in the sitting-room first. It sat in the middle of a massive oak fireplace, with brass shell-casings from the Great War standing at either end of the large mantelpiece.

It lit with a 'plop' and blazed up the bars, at first without emitting any heat whatsoever. The kitchenette was so cold that she filled the kettle and brought it back to the fireplace. In the hearth was a ring, which she lit, then placed the kettle on it.

The only food she could find was some sorry-looking apples, a couple of potatoes, a jar of home-made jam and a surprisingly large amount of butter in a dish in the meat safe. The bread-bin revealed a half-loaf and some crumpets.

When Bill returned he found her before the fire, coat off, wielding a large fork with a crumpet on its prongs, toasting before the bubbling gas-flames.

He looked down at her, at her slender legs curled close together at her side, her other arm supporting her weight on the floor. Her dress, draped around her lithe body, had ridden up above her knees.

Bill hunkered down, held her chin and gently lifted her mouth to his. When they parted, he took the fork from her other hand and laid it down.

Mary stood up before him, crossed her arms, took hold of the hem of her dress and pulled it over her head.

He watched as her slim figure, dressed in a white petticoat, stretched out above him.

Bill slumped to his knees, and placed his hands on her legs, ran them up, beyond the top of her stockings, on to the smooth skin of her thighs to the lacy edge of her knickers.

He drew them down to her knees, where they fluttered under their own weight to the floor. She stepped quickly out of them as Bill drew her to him, arms wrapped around her bottom, head on her belly whilst she ran her hands through his hair.

They stayed like that for some time before he drew back, gently lifted the hem of her petticoat and lightly kissed the soft skin of her belly, brushing his lips lower, reaching the fine hair that grew there.

Mary's breathing became ragged. She pulled suddenly away and sank to the floor. Bill dropped his pants and shorts as she put a cushion under her hips and freed her breasts.

She held up her arms and he sank down on her.

Their physical hunger after their separation drove them to a sudden frenzy.

Mary's breathing became ragged. She suddenly pulled away and sank to the floor. Holding up her arms she drew him down to her. Their physical hunger after the separation drove them into a frenzy, his actions that of an animal that knew it's only hope of immortality in a dangerous world was further life through this woman.

Afterwards, they fell violently apart, Mary rolling onto her face.

She had never before felt so alive.

Eventually Bill crawled to her, pulled her on to him and kissed her plastered hair, stroking it gently, tenderly, out of her eyes.

'I'm sorry.'

She put her finger to his lips,

'Shush, don't spoil it. You're a beast, my beast, and I love you.'

She got around at last to buttering the crumpets and spreading home-made strawberry jam from the WI on the tops. Two mugs of steaming hot tea completed their little supper.

Taking a deep breath Bill told her about the CO's refusal, and his petition to Wing Headquarters.

Mary sat back on her legs, soles of her feet sticking out behind her, both hands cupping her mug. Anxiously she asked: 'What happens if they don't give you permission, Bill?'

He shook his head. 'We'll find a way, don't you worry, and in any case after the war nothing can stop us.'

He paused, realized that that sounded so far away, and added: 'The move to France means I don't think it will be long now before it's all over, but we might not be able to see so much of each other for a while.' He wished he hadn't added that, though it needed to be said.

They lapsed into a miserable silence, broken only by the wireless, tuned low to the American Forces service. It was coming from the Granada Theatre in Bedford.

In the winter of 1944 there was, for many servicemen and women, in the music of Glenn Miller and the Band of the AEF a sort of hope, a glimpse of an ordinary life beyond the war: a magic spell born from the mouths of the golden saxophones and waving trombones, the steady resonance of the double basses, and the soft unstraining voices of the singers; it was timeless magic, and yet so much *of* their time.

After a while she whispered: 'I'm not a scientist, thank God. There is no conception of love in the physicist's universe.'

She raised herself and leant over him. Her head was framed in the faint light of the window, her hair hung down to touch his face. 'What is the point of our creation if this is all there is? Life for me is an interlude in a spiritual existence that was there before and will be after this life on earth. Should anything happen — we'll never be separated now — *ever.*'

Bill was taken unawares by her sudden seriousness, but then she was, after all, a 'bluestocking' as she called it, used no doubt to intellectual debate at the university about such matters.

He pulled her gently down to him and rocked her soothingly.

'No, we won't, will we. But I'll be all right darling — trust me. It's not as bad as you think.' Could she detect anything in his voice? In truth he wondered how long he could take it, how long he would be *around* to take it.

They slept at last, held in each other's arms.

Slept, as the sperm and the egg fused, the complete and final 'union' of their bodies; slept — while a new life grew in size and strength inside her, whilst thousands died in the ruins of ancient and once noble cities of Europe.

The Nazi empire was beginning, ever more rapidly, to crumble.

Sleep was still with them when in the warm dark morning bed they made love again, side by side, tenderly, equally, quietly, except for the melodic accompaniment of the springs of the old bed, which left them helpless with laughter when the seriousness of the business was done.

The crept like naughty children to the shared bathroom beneath the stairs, the giant wall-mounted copper geyser making noises that frankly scared him to death, made him fearful that an explosion was imminent.

Mary teased him. 'Don't you have these in that wonderful US of A you are always on about?'

He looked at her in disbelief. 'You got to be kidding. Looks like something the RAF boys drop over Berlin.'

Laughing and joking, they were sitting together in the bath, washing each other when someone tried the door handle several times.

Frozen, Mary called out: 'I won't be long.'

Bill added in an artificially deep voice: 'Just my back to do.'

They sniggered childish giggles as they heard a woman's voice say: 'Well, really,' and footsteps recede down the passage.

Dried, they donned the dressing-gowns found in the flat — both female. Mary was in a plain yellow towelling, Bill in a fetching pink silk affair with ruffles and feathers.

Creeping along, they were just at their doorway congratulating themselves on not being seen when they became aware of an elderly, military-looking gentleman, morning newspaper under his arm, a fierce eye behind his monocle, staring at them. He suddenly roared out: 'Damn Yankee pervert. Don't you know there's a war on?'

It was too much. Roaring with laughter they ran in and closed the door chanting: 'Don't you know there's a war on?'

In the bedroom Mary said, suggestively: 'The old boy is right — you do look very nice.'

He fluttered his eyes at her.

They made love yet again, a newly liberated Mary on top.

The fog was still about, but visibility was increasing. He called the operations room. All pilots had to be back on base by 2100 hours that evening.

The weather was expected to continue to improve and, with all planes in the squadron returned, offensive action was going to resume next day.

They had lunch in a British Restaurant. Something he'd never heard of, called shepherd's pie, with semolina as dessert, was being served.

He looked around at the wartime crowds, women in turbans and overalls, workers, clerks, shop-assistants, all queuing at the self-service counter, pushing their trays obediently along, not stopping as dollops of food on plates were pushed out by hairnetted women behind the banging, shouting, supply point. Tea was dispensed from huge metal kettles — whole rows of mugs were filled as the girl traversed them, pouring without stopping. Sing-along music blared out from loudspeakers.

'Why on earth did we come here?' he grumbled.

She grimaced. 'Best place for a square meal if you want it quickly. We can go to a pub later.'

He did as he was told, sitting in a corner, trying to look as inconspicuous as possible as Mary queued for both of them. Later, in an old Victorian pub with opaque glass windows, which was situated on a corner, they sat opposite each other in a booth. Mary sipped her drink, steeled herself 'Bill — we need to talk.'

'Darling, I know.'

For the moment that seemed to silence them both.

At last Bill relented. 'I'm asking one of the padres and the adjutant to have your address.' He shot out his hand to cover hers as her face began to crumple.

'Darling — darling — listen — it could be anything. But you want somebody to tell you what's happening, don't you?'

Miserably, fighting back the tears, she

nodded. Between sniffs she managed:

'Of course. I'm being silly. Forgive me.'

Bill frowned, hung his head.

'Anyway — that's what I'll do, and my parents — this is their address.' He opened his billfold, took out a card and gave it to her. 'I'm writing to tell them all about you, how we're going to be married as soon as possible — that I want them to look upon you as family right away.'

In the beginning their parting was almost matter-of-fact, both pretending to the other that everything was just fine. Bill said not to come to the station, but that was a step too far for Mary.

They walked slowly through an afternoon of gathering gloom, but the fog was nearly all gone. When it came time to say goodbye, they lingered so long, couldn't bear to part, that he nearly missed the train, had to run for it when the guard's shrill whistle got through to his senses.

She watched from the ticket-inspector's gate as he took the footbridge stairs two at a time. The carriages jerked, began to move as his face appeared at a window.

The ticket-inspector, seeing her misery, flicked his head. 'Come and stand through here.'

'Thank you.' She moved on to the platform opposite as Bill dropped the window.

'Take care,' she called.

'I will,' he answered. *'I love you.'*

But before she could respond the ground shook as the great clanking bulk of a freight train going in the opposite direction obscured all view of him.

By the time the fifteen low-loaders, each with a new tank on board, had ground past, the brake van finally hissing away into the night, his train had gone, the track opposite was empty.

Only the last section of it was still in sight as it disappeared around a bend, the red tail-light eventually extinguished from view.

Mary turned and thanked the inspector, who nodded sympathetically. A great dread filled her heart as she walked away. She hadn't been able to say she loved him.

# CHAPTER TEN

They were to support a raid on Stettin.

The weather was foul when they took off and it got steadily worse, the cloud thickening and cross-winds battering the ship as he climbed through 10,000 feet.

As they penetrated further into Germany the turbulence grew, and to make matters worse, icing started to occur. Short transmissions from other pilots indicated that some were aborting the mission because engines were running so rough that they couldn't stay in formation.

Bill expected the group leader to call it off, but no such order came. Cursing, he struggled with the controls, worried that any moment the turbulence would hit so hard that the artificial horizon would topple — then he'd be in big shit in this cloud.

Abruptly the radio crackled with an urgent voice. 'Cowboy Green section to Horseback. Bandits all around, seventy plus. Are you receiving, Horseback?'

Cowboy was one of the unseen bomber formations. Horseback was the escorts.

The radio continued to crackle on.

'We're in clear sky — looks like they're coming down for a head-on attack.'

Almost immediately combat messages started to jam the airways. One desperate wit said it all.

'Jeez — the whole frigging *Luftwaffe*'s out to get me.'

At that moment the order for the bombers to turn back was given at last, since the thick clouds and general confusion precluded any effective hit on the target.

The group leader's voice came over the airways: 'Horseback one calling all Mustangs — let's go help Cowboy.'

Bill took his formation to the right, eventually breaking cloud to find themselves right in the middle of the mess.

The Germans had put up everything they could, including twin-engined Me110s and Dornier 217s. They were fighting with desperation and immense courage to defend their homeland — just like the RAF boys in the Battle of Britain.

Bill led the attack down on a gaggle of 110s, which immediately went into a defensive circle so that each one covered the other's tail.

Bill went in head-on, and saw hits on one 110, which broke away. He was lining up for a second shot when another Mustang cut in front of him and sent it down in a flaming dive. From then on, like all the others, he was turning and twisting, sweating and cursing as he fought more to stay alive than anything else.

The Germans were firing rocket salvos into the massed formations. Airplanes, American and German, were going down in every direction, gas-tanks burning with intense orange flames, streaming like great fiery rockets towards the earth. And then, as so often happened, the sky was empty, leaving only an awful spectacle to strain his shattered nerves. Someone, German or American, there was no way of telling, had taken to his 'chute. He drifted slowly, swinging gently from side to side — on fire, his body emitting flame and smoke like the kid's dummy he'd seen on a daylight bonfire in England. The flames licked up the shroud lines and started on the canopy. Mercifully it folded up, and the blackened corpse fell away to earth, was lost from sight.

His engine sounded rough. Bill checked his altitude.

The instrument showed 25,000 feet. He

radioed his problem and turned for home, soon joined by two others from the same squadron.

The cylinder-head temperature gauge started to climb steadily. Bill's mouth felt as dry as sandpaper, but he remembered how one of the guys had told him he'd got back by enriching the fuel mixture, which helped the engine run cool. Keeping as much altitude as possible, he followed the Kiel Canal to the coast at Schleswig-Holstein.

Nervously, Bill ran his swollen tongue over cracked lips. Only the North Sea to get across now.

The others began weaving over him. Bill told them to leave — they would need all their fuel. 'Go home — I'll be OK. I'll call Air-Sea Rescue.'

He looked down at the expanse of water. It looked flat, but he could just see white flecks. Bill knew that down there it was probably running a heavy sea. Rescue would be most unlikely.

One of them flew his ship under his and appeared on the other side.

'How's it look?' Bill asked.

When there was no reply Bill suddenly realized what was going on. He flicked over to the emergency 'May Day' channel. As he suspected, the man was talking to rescue giving Bill's altitude and heading, and adding, 'There's oil everywhere — he's not gonna make it. He'll have to bail out soon.'

'Can he give us a long transmission so we can get a fix on him?' said a clipped, steady English voice.

Bill butted in. He meant it to sound flippant, although his heart was in his boots, so what came out of his mouth took him by surprise.

' 'Course I can. Mary had a little lamb. . . .'

*Mary.* Oh god Mary.

He made an effort, dragged himself back to the task in hand and finished the rhyme, then repeated it over until the English voice said: 'That's fine. You're a long way out and the weather conditions are bad but we'll do our best. Good luck.'

Bill waved the others away. All alone, he was left with his thoughts of Mary. Would he ever see her again? Mercifully he had to keep a tight watch on his instruments, on the temperature, the altitude and heading. It didn't allow for such terrible thoughts.

He was making for Martlesham Heath airfield by Ipswich on the east coast. Halfway across and he was down to 9,000 feet. He was flying on the proverbial wing and a prayer.

At 2,000 feet he reckoned he should be sighting land, but all he could see was grey blending into darker grey. At 1,800 — still nothing. The prayer increased.

At 1,600 — *something:* a low dark line. Bill strained forward, on the edge of his seat. Slowly the sandy marshland of Orfordness came into view, but at this angle of approach he was sinking too fast, he would never make it. When he eased the stick as far back as he dared, the plane began to shudder, on the point of stalling.

He nudged it fractionally forward again, aware that there was less than 600 feet between him and the winding estuary below. Bill was preparing to belly-in when he suddenly saw the strip was dead ahead. He dropped the undercarriage, prayed it would get down in time, and heard it thump home just as he eased the stick back, cleared the boundary fence and dropped heavily on to the grass. When he rolled to a halt, Bill sagged in his straps, did nothing until his heart, literally banging in his chest, finally slowed down.

Wearily he slid back the hood, unstrapped and climbed out on to the wing. He pulled off his helmet and ran his hand through his wet hair. The crash truck found him, relieving himself against the hedge.

He flew back later that afternoon, getting in just before dusk — risky, as most flying had to be completed an hour before sunset to minimize misidentifications.

The crew chief was looking worried.

'What happened, sir?'

Bill patted his ship's nose. 'Went all temperamental on me — oil loss.'

He was debriefed by an Intelligence Officer in his hut, had his slug of whisky and was about to go for a shower when an orderly found him.

'Sir, Lieutenant *Riley* at Wing headquarters has been trying to reach you all day. Says he's going to be in the office late if you'd like to see him.'

Bill forgot about the shower. Still in his leather flying-jacket he knocked and entered Riley's room. Riley was at a bookcase consulting a text. He looked up.

'Hi there.'

Bill wasted no time.

'What have you got?'

Riley put the book back on to the shelf.

'You won't believe it.'

'Try me.'

'Your petition went through channels to General Spaatz, but he's Stateside on R and R.'

Bill groaned. 'That's it then — we've got

189

to wait?'

'Not entirely.'

'What do you mean — who else can it go to? He's the top.'

Light flashed off Riley's glasses as he leant back, clearly enjoying himself.

'I got in touch with Colonel Clark — he's the legal adviser to US Forces in Europe and. . . .'

Bill began to be irritated. It had been a hell of a day.

'Come on.'

'OK. Currently your application to marry Mary Rice is on the way to SHAEF HQ, to no less a person than Ike himself. You should get a reply in twenty-four hours.'

Bill felt as if the ground had opened up and he was about to be swallowed.

'Ike? Now? With all that's going down?'

Riley nodded. 'Yep. He still insists on getting through all the day-to-day running of *his* army — when he can.'

Bill left the office in a daze, not sure he wasn't hallucinating from fatigue and stress.

Mary pored over the transcripts. Something in the phrasing was not right, not making sense, at least not to her. She played with it for half an hour or so, then dug out a manuscript from an earlier intercept. At last

190

she realized what it was that was bothering her.

She found Sir George in the canteen, sedately sipping his tea. He looked up in surprise. 'Doctor Rice. Is there a problem?'

'I think you need to come back to the hut, Sir George. The whole meaning of one of the transcripts to the *Waffen SS* takes on a new slant if you restructure the sentence — the punctuation, that is. The operator was from southern Germany.'

He knew Mary was not one to exaggerate, so he finished his tea less sedately, folded *The Times* and stood up.

'Very well. Lead on, MacDuff.'

Back in the hut, on the main table where they could lay out the work under a low suspended light taken from a billiard table, she took him through what she had found.

Afterwards, Sir George stayed motionless. After some moments he straightened up.

'I'm going to take this upstairs — see what they make of it.' Sir George's little moustache received a brush with a finger. 'Whatever they say, very good work indeed, Doctor Rice.'

Flushed with the praise, generous indeed from Sir George, Mary said she'd be in the canteen if he needed her. She'd been very hungry recently.

He didn't come and fetch her, but was waiting for her in his little cubicle of an office with the door open. He called to her as she entered the hut.

'Close the door behind you.'

He indicated a chair. As she took it she asked: 'Is this about the translation?'

Sir George nodded.

'They're very pleased with you. As you know, intelligence work is like putting together a jigsaw when you haven't got a complete set and guessing what's in the blank spaces. Well, my dear, I'm pleased to tell you that what you construed from that passage of German fitted one of those spaces. I'm not permitted, of course, to give you the full picture, and indeed, they don't tell me any more than I need to know, but it was an invaluable pointer and they are delighted. They have asked me to thank you personally. Your name is being forwarded to some committee or other that might one day see you honoured for your services.'

Mary was flabbergasted. Sensing the interview was over she started to rise but he motioned her down. 'Care to join me in a celebratory snifter?'

He swivelled in his chair and, with a set of keys, opened a little mahogany wall-cabinet, and produced two cut glasses and a bottle of sherry. Setting them on the desk top he delicately poured out the dark tawny liquid that seemed to sparkle with the sun that had been part of its birth.

As a way of explanation he said; 'I've had this bottle since nineteen forty — only toast our little victories in this department with it.'

He handed her one of the glasses.

'Well done. Let's hope that's another step, however small, to the end of this beastly affair.'

Mary nodded as they touched glasses.

'Please God.'

Even as they spoke, Bletchley Park was warning SHAEF HQ of a strange request for American-accented English-speaking troops to be sent immediately away from the main front line, to near the quiet Ardennes sector.

But Mary's work, by its very nature a secondary intelligence evaluation, was already being overtaken by events.

Those 'American'-speaking soldiers, equipped with American Jeeps, uniforms and weapons, were already behind Allied lines.

General Dwight D. Eisenhower had just finished some routine paper work when the first news came in of the Germans'

Ardennes offensive.

The weather all over northern Europe was bad, with low cloud-bases, freezing fog — and snow.

News trickled through to the squadron of the German offensive, and the inability of the Allied Tactical Air Force to intervene.

Men were mooching about, uneasy, the taken-for-granted victory suddenly less sure, at least in the near future, all plans, all dreams, on hold.

They were all raging with frustration that they couldn't get into the fight, even from England. Weather was predicted to be bad for days — even longer, with heavy snow-falls.

Bill, with his large overcoat on, was stretched out on his bunk writing a letter to Mary when a knock came on the door.

He looked up. 'Come in.'

Riley stood there.

'You guys not flying for Uncle Sam today?'

Bill, suddenly tense on seeing Riley, still managed: 'No. Has the weather escaped you in that fine warm room of yours?'

Riley opened his greatcoat and shook and stamped off some of the snow.

*'Touché.'*

But Bill was already swinging his legs to

the floor and standing up.

'Well?'

Riley moved to the window, looked out at the drifting snow. 'You going to try to see Mary? This isn't going to ease up for days, is it?'

Impatiently, Bill said: 'Just waiting for a general stand-down to be announced.' He paused, then added: 'Are you trying to let me down gently or what? I don't have you down as a sadist.'

Riley slid his hand into a pocket and produced a message sheet.

'Just got this.' He unfolded it, cleared his throat and read:

'From Supreme Headquarters, Allied Expeditionary Force, to First Lieutenant William Anderson USAAF. You have permission to marry Miss Mary Rice — no one else.'

Riley looked up, smiled and finished: 'Signed, *personally,* Dwight D. Eisenhower, Supreme Commander SHAEF.'

Bill let out one terrific yell, grabbed Riley and danced around shouting: 'Riley, you genius, you're the greatest lawyer on earth. Come to the club — drinks on me.'

When the initial euphoria was past and he

let go of Riley, the latter said: 'You may not be popular with the CO of your squadron.'

Bill grinned. 'He'll be fine. If we get a forty-eight I'll be married before he even knows it — and with this . . .' he took the message from Riley's fingers . . . 'he can hardly complain.'

His face suddenly clouded. 'Say — can we marry in a civil office — *quickly?*'

Riley shrugged. 'If that's what your lady wants, I'm sure I can fix it.'

Bill held his arms wide. 'Riley, is there no end to your talents?'

Neither of them could know that forty years later Riley would be a Supreme Court judge.

Mary was on High Table, dining with the Master and Fellows when the door at the far end burst open. At the clamour, everybody stopped eating, looked around, down the two long candlelit rows of tables to the entrance where Bill, with the porter hanging on to his arm, stood shouting:

'Mary, Mary . . . Marry me. Ike himself has given us permission.'

Startled she dropped her spoon, said to the Master: 'I'm sorry . . . I must. . . .'

The goatee-bearded patrician, the foremost authority on ancient Persia in the land, laid a hand on her arm.

'My dear, his name?'

Mary gulped. 'Bill Anderson, Master, he is a lieutenant in the American Air Force.'

The Master waved. 'Lieutenant Anderson — please come and join us.'

There was a ripple of surprise. College servants scrambled to set another place as one of the Fellows moved to let Bill sit beside her.

Bill strode up the hall, stepped up on to the platform on which was the High Table.

The Master rose to meet him and took his hand, smiling and introducing Mary.

'I think you already know Doctor Rice?'

Bill looked into her eyes.

'I do, sir. And I await her reply. Will you marry me — on this leave — right away?'

One could almost hear a pin drop in the centuries-old hall.

Unintentionally she kept him waiting several seconds until she could trust her voice.

'I will.'

Cheering, the students threw all their napkins in the air as the Master warmly clasped them both on their shoulders.

Later, when they were walking on their own, with her arm through his, they talked and talked like the excited youngsters they were.

Suddenly serious, Mary said: 'Bill, can we get to see my parents — I really want you to meet them?'

'Sure, honey — tomorrow — OK? Is it far?'

She squeezed his arm. 'Thank you, darling. No, we can do it in a day. But I'm feeling guilty about your mum and dad.'

Wistfully Bill shook his head.

'I daren't cable them — they would get such a fright, thinking it was from the War Department. Anyway, there is no rush. I can tell them more about you in a letter — enclose a photo.'

Mary winced. 'Do you think they'll be upset? I mean, they don't know anything about me — probably think I'm a little English gold-digger or something.'

Bill gave a snort.

'No way. They trust me. I'm a big boy now.'

She stopped dead.

'How old are you, Bill?'

'Twenty-one last March — and you?'

She looked sheepish. 'You sure you want to marry an older woman?'

He pulled a face. 'Hell, that *bad?*'

She nodded. 'Afraid so, I'm twenty-two.'

He slapped his forehead.

'I knew it. You'll be old and I'll still be young and handsome.'

She gave him a punch.

They resumed their walk in the snow.

'We'll need to catch an early train, and change at Bedford. My parents live in St Albans.'

'Right.'

It meant nothing to him.

When they reached her digs he started to chuckle.

'What's funny?'

He gestured at the terraced house. 'You're there — me in my place. Where are we going to meet — *tonight?*'

Mary rolled her eyes. 'My God, what am I letting myself in for?'

Bill winked suggestively.

At Bedford they waited on the platform of the red-brick Victorian station that served the main line to London. It was packed with GIs and RAF types, and some giggling girls. Dust blew up into their eyes from the unswept, stone-slabbed platform that elevated them above the greasy, litter-strewn track.

They made their way to the refreshment room, queued for two thick, cracked cups of stewed tea, and two rock-cakes from a woman who drew boiling water into a large kettle from a chromium-plated urn.

She proceeded to fill more rows of cups with a continuous stream of the thick dark fluid as they moved on to a woman at the till, whose wobbling cigarette was stuck to her lower lip. She checked their tray, then said: 'Eightpence, luv,' and pressed the keys of the till.

The charge came up, printed on cards inside the glass window of the machine. Bill proffered half a crown and waited for his change as Mary went to look for seats. They were all taken, so they faced each other, using the window-ledge to park their cups.

Mary tried to break off a piece of cake, found it hard going. She pulled a face, and pushed the plate away. 'Bill, I'd better warn you — my father isn't easy these days. He's always in a lot of pain. He was blown up at Dunkirk — lost a leg.'

Bill winced. 'Hell, I'm sorry — I had no idea. I thought you said he was a printer.'

She nodded. 'He was, before the war. He was in the BEF. It's just that he'll have a go at you — but honestly he's really very nice, when you get to know him properly.'

He smiled. 'He's your father — that's enough for me.'

She leaned forward and gave him a kiss

on the cheek.

'I love you.'

A great clatter of boots on the stone outside took their attention. Khaki uniforms were everywhere, together with steel helmets, gas-masks, kit-bags and rifles. Mary noticed the faces of the soldiers, young and soft with the contours of boyhood; the sergeants were older, their skin leathery and creased.

Bill said: 'Looks like a unit on the move. This train is going to be very crowded.'

They couldn't see the black, dirty engine when it drew in, only the hissing steam as it rumbled past, shaking the ground. In a scream of tortured metal on metal it ground to a halt at the end of the platform. Doors opened, the crowds on the platform pushing forward even before it stopped.

Shaking his head, Bill said: 'We'll never get on that.'

Mary's eyes flashed. 'Oh, yes we will.'

They downed the remainder of their teas, left the rock-cakes and rushed out on to the steam-filled platform.

Mary led the way, found a door at the end of a corridor coach. People were standing in the entrance, apparently unable to go any further.

She got up on to the step and began pushing her way in. Embarrassed, Bill apologized as he followed her into the gloomy corridor, then continued on down its length, all the while shouldering past people and climbing over cases. Half-way along there was a little more space. She leant against the window rail, with Bill hard up against her. He smiled and mimed a kiss. Mary giggled. 'You can try but somehow I don't think it's going to work.'

The carriage smelt of a mixture of engine smoke, cigarette smoke and the dampness of thick serge, and was obviously rarely cleaned.

They remained stationary, packed like cattle in trucks, watching as more troops arrived and went into the station buffet. Feet scuffed on the carriage floor, voices rose in volume, and coughing and roars of laughter came from somewhere.

The train's eventual departure was presaged by several shrill blasts of the guard's whistle, the slamming of more doors, and a sudden jerk that would have sent everybody sprawling, if they had not all been jammed so tightly together. Brown suitcases and kitbags rained down on the people in the compartments.

To begin with they hardly went more than a walking-pace, lurching over points, trundling slowly over a steel bridge. Bill looked up the length of the River Ouse at the town of Bedford nestling on its banks as it had since early Danish settlements. He knew that John Bunyan had written his *Pilgrim's Progress* from a cell in the town jail.

The train, almost imperceptibly gathered momentum, the engine labouring with poor coal and the grossly overloaded carriages.

Eventually they cleared Bedford, headed south towards London across the flat brick-fields with the groups of tall chimneys dominating the skyline.

They plunged into a tunnel. Mary felt his mouth on her nose, tilted her face so that their lips met.

Smoke and steam swirled in through an open window. With a shout somebody grabbed the hanging leather strap and hauled it shut.

When they lunged out into the daylight again Bill chuckled. A dark spot had drifted on to the tip of her nose. With difficulty he got to his handkerchief and rubbed it away.

She giggled. 'Thank you, kind sir, but you need it too.'

She took the handkerchief and did the same to his forehead and cheek.

The journey was tedious, with many stops and always with the same agonizingly slow resumption from each station. Mary began to feel very tired.

At last they steamed into St Albans. Not many got out. The packed train was still standing at the platform long after they had left the station, crossed over a road bridge, and hand in hand walked out of sight of the railway.

She glanced up at him as they turned into her road. 'You're still sure about this Bill? Don't take any offence at anything Dad says will you? He doesn't mean it really.'

'I won't. Hell, he can't be that bad.'

But he was wrong.

The home was an Edwardian red-brick semi, the dwarf wall that had separated it from the road was now without its iron railing, only the stumps remaining after it had been taken for the war effort.

They stood in the porch, its floor tiled in red and blue, the blue-painted door divided by two panels of coloured glass.

He nervously fingered his tie as the sound of footsteps came on the wooden floor on the other side of the door.

It was opened, and a petite woman stood there, dressed in a blue cardigan and jumper, with a single string of pearls and a tartan skirt.

To Bill, her resemblance to Mary was

startling.

Her eyes fell on her daughter, and in a second they were hugging each other, the woman saying: 'Oh darling, it's wonderful to see you.'

Mary replied: 'And you too, Mummy.'

It was only after they had hugged again that Mrs Rice said worriedly: 'You're looking tired, are you overdoing it?'

Mary shook her head. 'No more than anybody else these days. At least I'm not in a factory, thank God.'

It was only then that her mother turned to Bill, who had stood patiently to one side, enjoying the warmth between them.

Mary introduced him. 'This is Bill, Mum.'

Mrs Rice held out her hand. 'It's nice to meet you. Mary has told us all about you.'

Bill took her hand, found it freezing cold as he shot a glance at Mary. 'I hope it wasn't all bad?'

Mary moved to her mother's side, put an arm around her shoulder.

'Never you mind. What goes on between a daughter and her mother is sacrosanct. Isn't that so, Mum?'

Mrs Rice patted Mary's hand. 'It was all good, Bill, I promise, and we think what you are doing is very brave.'

Bill winced, and shook his head.

'If you could see me sometimes. . . .'

When her mother had said 'we', Mary had released her hand, her face clouding as she asked: 'How's Dad?'

Mrs Rice tried to smile, but it didn't really succeed.

'Oh, much the same. The doctor has given him some different tablets for the pain. They seem to be working better. Come on in, he's in the garden — always did like snow, like a little boy.'

Bill followed the women into the hall from which stairs led straight up, the red carpet held by brass rods at the start of each riser. There was an oak hall table and hatrack, on which he hung his cap.

They walked down the passageway beside the stairs, passing a door that led into a room with a comfortable but threadbare sofa and two chairs grouped around a tiled fire-place. A bookcase and a standard lamp of turned mahogany completed the furnishings.

They passed another door on the same side, revealing a room with a wooden dining-table and four chairs, and a matching sideboard with photographs.

'Mind the step.'

He ducked his head as they entered a narrow kitchen with a gas-cooker and a shallow white sink with a water-heater above it. From there they passed into a small wash-room, similar to that at the cottage, which Mary referred to as the scullery. It contained a mangle with its smooth wooden rollers, one on top of the other, and a long geared handle to turn them with, and a round, gas-fired clothes-boiler. A washboard stood in the corner. A smell of dampness pervaded the room.

Then they finally stepped out into a long, thin strip of a garden with a concrete path running its length.

There was a figure of a man in a wheel-chair, his back to them, wearing a coat and with a rug over his knees.

They approached, Mrs Rice leading the way. She stood in front of the chair.

'Dear — Mary's here, and she's got Bill with her.'

Mary knelt down, and threw her arms around her father.

'Daddy.'

Bill stood beside her, still unable to see the man's face. He heard the voice of Mr Rice before anything else.

When Mary drew back he found himself looking down into eyes he already knew. There could be no doubt from which par-ent Mary had inherited them. Under dark eyebrows they stared back up at him, resentment already present even before he had opened his mouth. His nose was large, his thrusting jaw ended in a cleft chin. A once handsome face was now tinged with sadness, with defeat.

'So, this is your American?'

He managed to make 'American' sound like an insult.

Bill held out his hand.

'Pleased to meet you, sir'

Grudgingly a large hand took it.

'Always the polite ones, especially when they want to marry your daughter.'

'Oh John, don't be so rude.'

Mrs Rice sounded anxious, as though she had been expecting it.

Undeterred, Bill produced a bag of food he'd scrounged from one of the mess hall sergeants.

'Not only polite, sir, but I thought I might bribe you with food for your daughter's hand.'

The eyebrows furrowed. 'Clever with it as well, eh? But you know what they say. . . .'

Bill nodded wearily. 'Yes. Oversexed, overpaid, and over here — right?'

'That's right.' There was a note of triumph in John Rice's voice.

Mrs Rice took the bag. 'Oh, Bill, that's

very generous of you. Really, you shouldn't have done it.'

She shot a glance at her husband. 'We girls need to talk.'

Mary bent down and ostensibly gave her Father a hug, but whispered fiercely into his ear: 'Be good Daddy — for me.'

The two men were left alone together. Bill shifted from one foot to the other.

'Very nice family you have, sir.'

Mr Rice grunted, tried to move, pushing at the wheels of his chair which slipped in the snow, failing to grip.

Bill went to help, but was waved off with a testy: 'I can manage, thank you.'

Mr Rice got himself on to a part of the concrete path that had been swept clear of the snow and wheeled himself along to its end. Bill followed, not knowing what else to do.

At last Mr Rice said: 'How old are you?'

Bill lied, added a few months. 'Twenty-one and a half, sir.'

Mr Rice shook his head. 'I thought so. You're just a boy.'

Irritated, Bill drew himself up.

'Old enough, according to Uncle Sam.'

Mary's father grimaced. 'My family has already paid a heavy price in this war. Did Mary tell you about our boy? Went down in the Channel during the Battle of Britain. You Yanks weren't around then.'

Bill was flabbergasted. 'She never told me.'

Mr Rice took no notice, carried on. 'Her telling us about you, and getting wed came as a hell of a shock I can tell you. We had her down as a dyed-in-the-wool academic — thought she might never get married. And you — a *pilot*.' He shook his head. 'She was very close to Mark. Now look. . . .'

His shoulders slumped. 'This war will just about finish this family I can tell you.'

A silence descended as Bill still thought about Mary's brother.

Suddenly Mr Rice said: 'The women have got a lot to talk about. Care for a pint? There's a pub at the end of the road.'

Surprised and relieved, Bill straightened up. 'I sure would.'

They went out through the back gate, the wheelchair bumping along down an unmade lane, at the bottom of which was a small pub. They went into the door on the corner, marked 'Public Bar'. There was a counter with pump-handles, and a few mismatched tables and chairs clustered on the sawdust-sprinkled floor.

Several men were inside. They turned to look at Bill in his uniform, which stood out in the dingy surroundings. John Rice wheeled himself across the room, Bill irrationally noticing the tyre tracks in the sawdust. He slapped his hand on the bar top.

'Two pints of your best bitter, Mavis. . . .'

The buxom barmaid eyed Bill appreciatively as she began her work, pulling the handle and releasing the gurgling beer into the mugs which she held at an angle. Every time the handle sprang back upright there was a dull thud. Eventually she set the two glasses of frothing beer down on to the mats and took the coins John Rice proffered. He passed one to Bill and took the other himself.

'Cheers.'

Bill responded in kind.

After the first quaff John Rice wiped his mouth with the back of his hand and addressed the room.

'This is . . . what did you say your rank was, son?'

Bill obliged sheepishly. 'First lieutenant.'

'This is First Lieutenant Bill Anderson, soon to be my son-in-law, and he is currently kicking the shite out of the Hun in his own backyard.'

The other men nodded or called out greetings of one sort or another. Bill held up his beer in salute, then drank long and deep. When he lowered his glass it was to find, for the first time, John Rice grinning at him.

'It's been that bad, eh?'

'What do you mean?'

'Meeting me.'

Ruefully Bill ran a hand through his hair. 'Shall we just say that I was worried that you probably wouldn't like me.'

John Rice looked down into his glass. 'I haven't been easy to live with these last couple of years, Bill, I don't mind admitting.'

He gazed sadly at the wheelchair. 'Never thought I'd end up in one of these.'

They moved to a corner. Bill pulled away a chair to allow John Rice to get close to the table, and set down his beer.

They sat back, drinking in silence for a moment as the murmur of the voices in the bar returned to normal. At last John Rice said, in a lowered tone: 'I've had nobody around here I could talk to, nobody who could understand. . . .'

He dropped his gaze. 'I was terrified.'

Bill, taken unawares, said nothing, then realized that his future father-in-law was waiting expectantly, that he was being given a rare opportunity, that Mary's father had started to bare his soul to him.

He swallowed hard, said aloud, to the only person in the world he'd admitted it to before — even, he realized, to himself:

'If you must know, I turned back on a mission, radioed there was a problem, when really there wasn't. Nothing was ever said, but at that moment I just couldn't do it.' He shook his head. 'I was overcome with fear, intense, nauseating fear.' He shuddered. 'You don't know how bad it's going to be until you're buckling in on the day. That's when it gets you — dread sits in your stomach like a cold dead animal. Most days you can get on top of it, but sometimes . . .' His voice tailed away.

The older man looked into the younger man's eyes, and in that instant a bond was formed.

Mary came in from the garden, frowning.

'They're not there.'

Mrs Rice, laying the dining-room table, paused with a fork in her hand. 'Oh dear, I expect they've gone down to the King's Arms. Your father goes there quite a lot nowadays.'

Mary came and stood by her. 'Mummy, are you trying to tell me something?'

Mrs Rice's lower lip trembled, and tears came into her eyes.

'Oh, mother. . . .'

That did it. Mrs Rice turned to her daughter, who cuddled her as great sobs racked her body.

'There, there. . . .'

It all came out. John Rice had been hell to live with, and had taken to going daily to the King's Arms at lunch-times and then again most evenings. She'd had to put up with a lot of loneliness, and then being with a husband who vacillated between gruffness and great periods of brooding introspection.

'Damn. Damn this whole bloody mess. It's killed my son, it's ruined our health, it's . . . ruined our life.'

Mary had never heard her mother swear before. Almost immediately Mrs Rice dabbed at her eyes with a little bordered handkerchief.

'I'm sorry, Mary — don't take any notice of me — *please.* Dad's all right really. Don't let it worry you on your day tomorrow. Really, I'm all right — just being stupid.'

Upset, Mary cuddled her again.

'Don't be silly, Mum. Is it the wheelchair? Is that what he can't come to terms with?'

'No.'

She felt her mother's head move from side to side. 'No, no. Something happened in

France — when he was injured. He won't talk about it.'

Frightened, Mary hugged her mother, rocking back and forth.

The 'something' that had been eating away at John Rice was now known to Bill Anderson. It was an incident that had lasted less than thirty seconds.

In the heat of battle, on the outskirts of a village, a soldier in his platoon had been injured while the platoon was in a forward defensive position. They had come under heavy mortar fire. The man had screamed for help, but John Rice had found himself unable to move, frozen to the ground in terror. It had only ended when there had been a whoosh, the man's head had been sliced off and John Rice had found himself staring at somebody's bloody leg. Then he had realized it was his.

Bill took the empty glasses in one hand. Before he moved to the counter he put his other hand on the older man's shoulder. 'Anybody who's been there knows. You do your best. Sometimes it's more than enough — sometimes it's not enough. War is not logical. War is crap.'

Mary and her mother had restored themselves to a sad calmness. There was still no

215

sign of the menfolk. Their eyes met. Mary said: 'Shall I go down and get them?'

Her mother was adamant. 'Leave them alone, dear, your father will come home in his own sweet time.'

Mary raised an eyebrow. 'What do you think is happening? I'm worried for Bill.'

There was a sudden shout from the direction of the garden. Mary and her mother watched in horror as a charging Bill, pushing John Rice in his wheelchair, tore up the path, weaving dangerously from side to side until in an explosion of snow the chair went sideways and rolled over. Its occupant was flung out and Bill fell on top of him.

Shocked, the women ran to help, appalled at the twisted bodies and still-spinning wheels. When they got there they pulled up abruptly and stared down in amazement.

The two men were shaking with laughter, tears streaming down their faces. When at last he caught his breath John Rice looked up at his wife, and for the first time in recent memory, she saw again the man she had married.

Then Bill and he giggled like kids, and the women realized that they were both heavily under the influence.

But her mother's relief was so overwhelming that Mary's anger at Bill evaporated.

Mother and daughter hugged each other as they joined tearfully in the laughter.

John Rice looked up at his daughter and wagged a finger. 'You've got yourself a good one here, Mary — even if he is a Yank. You take care of him now, or you'll have me to answer to.'

Mary looked at Bill and raised an eyebrow. With mock severity she said: 'Oh, I'll take good care of him all right.'

They enjoyed a wonderful evening. Mary had never known her parents to be so happy.

When the time came to leave the atmosphere became more sober. Her mother was growing tearful again, but with happiness.

'We'll be thinking of you both.'

'I'm so sorry you can't be there,' Mary said sadly, 'but it's the only place we can do it really quickly, and Bill will have to return to the Air Force almost immediately.'

Her father patted her hand. 'We understand, gal — all we want is your happiness. Anyway it's not as though these are normal times eh?'

Her mother nodded. 'That's right, Mary dear, yours and Bill's happiness.'

They stood in the hall, Mrs Rice with her hand on the blackout curtain, her other around Mary. The two women held on to each other for as long as possible as they talked.

The men made their own farewells. There was no exhortation to glory or the destruction of the enemy by John Rice.

They grasped hands as he said: 'You take care of yourself, son, for Mary's sake — and ours. No heroics, now.'

'No heroics, Dad — that's a promise.'

They finally left, kissing and shaking hands again in the dark of the front garden. Her parents were still there, despite the cold as they gave a last wave and turned the corner.

Down the next street the moon was riding between wildly scudding clouds, bright between the roofs and chimneys.

Mary had an arm around his waist, one of his was about her shoulders.

'Bill.' She suddenly stopped, the moonlight glowed on her upturned face.

'Darling, I love you.' It was said very seriously. He kissed her on her forehead.

'Now, that's what I like to hear — but why now?'

'Oh, for what you did back there.'

'You mean your father?'

'Yes.'

'Your old man is OK — one of the best.'

She was going to say something more, but

he kissed her, long and hard.

They didn't even notice a couple of giggling girls, arm-in-arm, who passed by and called out: 'That's it Yank, give her one. There's two more here when you've finished.'

They were married by special licence next day at Cambridge Register Office. Bill slid the ring on her third finger, left hand, just after 11 a.m.

They dined at a reserved table at the Garden House Hotel, walked along the Backs, managed to get a punt despite the winter's day — the old boatman, on hearing they were just married, got it out especially for them, and insisted on poling as they lay side by side under blankets. He joined them in a toast from the hip flask that Bill proffered to him.

'Long life and happiness together.'

After supper they sat before a crackling log-fire in the lounge, watching the world go by. It was Christmas Eve, 1944.

Glenn Miller was due to broadcast to America later — from Paris.

Mary sprawled in a leather chair, holding a brandy in one hand, her arm languidly outstretched. The flames of the fire were reflected in the glass of the balloon. She murmured: 'Darling, this is the happiest day of my life.'

Bill sat opposite her, swirling the brandy in his glass as he held it cupped in both hands.

'Mary *Anderson* . . .' he grinned and paused deliberately. Her heart leapt at the sound of her new name.

'Mary Anderson — you are a beautiful woman. I have no idea why you have married me, but you have made me the proudest, happiest man on earth.'

They raised their glasses to each other. Mary thought for a while, then, biting her lip, said, 'Bill. . . .'

He looked from the fire back to her. When she didn't immediately continue, he suddenly realized that she was finding it difficult. His voice quickened. 'What?'

She took a quick sip of her brandy. 'I didn't want to spoil your day — I didn't know how you'd take it but. . . .'

Bill frowned. 'What's up? What's wrong?'

'Nothing's wrong — but well — I'm expecting. . . .'

Bill sat so unmoving that for a second she didn't think he had understood her.

To be certain she added. 'I'm due some time in July — maybe August.'

Bill suddenly stood up, put his drink down

and came over and sat on the leather arm of her chair. Pulling her to him he kissed the top of her head and whispered, 'Darling — that's wonderful. How long have you known?'

Mary blushed. 'Soon after our stay at the flat I knew that something *might* have happened.'

'Have you been to see the doctor?'

She nodded. 'Two days ago — everything was fine.' She chuckled. 'He said he'd seen more unmarried young ladies in the family way in the last four years than in the previous forty.'

Bill kissed her head again.

'Well, you're *Mrs* Anderson, expecting our first, and that's terrific.'

Mary blushed. 'I never in a million years thought that I'd be with child on my *wedding* night of all nights. I couldn't tell Mum and Dad — but I will soon.'

Bill hunched down in front of her and looked up. 'Mary, we knew from the very beginning we were made for each other. Now you are an old married woman, and though I didn't think it possible I love you even more.'

She ruffled his hair with her hand.

'Husband — my husband.'

They were just going to bed when the rumour began to circulate through the servicemen crowded into the bar. Somebody said that the news had come across with a group of bomber boys from the Three-O-Six stationed at Thurleigh near Bedford.

Glenn Miller's plane to Paris had gone missing some ten days previously — the news was only now leaking out. A hush came over the place. What with the Battle of the Bulge still raging, the new V2 rockets causing terror, and now this, the year of 1944 was ending on a very gloomy note after the euphoria of the summer and autumn.

Victory in Europe suddenly seemed further away than ever.

# CHAPTER ELEVEN

They sat at breakfast, not speaking much. Bill had to return to the squadron. The honeymoon was over.

The weather was breaking, there was a lot for the Air Force to do. It was business as usual.

Bill looked out at the now sun-kissed snow, and the clear blue sky.

'I want you to stay here, Mary, don't come to the station.'

She started to protest but he would have none of it. 'I'm getting a ride with some of the guys — and I don't want you walking around in this, it's icy underfoot.'

She lapsed into a miserable silence, picked at her food.

All too soon they were finished, and some boisterous yelling from the direction of the lobby indicated that the others were ready to go.

Bill took both of her hands in his. 'Now

we're married you're official — *Mrs* Anderson. You call the squadron office whenever you feel like it.'

She bit her lower lip to stop it from quivering. 'When will I see you again, Bill?'

Sadly he shook his head. 'That's not something I can say with certainty.'

Mary continued to look glum, so he tried to cheer her up. 'Don't worry, everything is going to be all right. You take good care of yourself — and that little girl of mine.'

Mary looked at him in surprise. 'Little girl?'

He grinned. 'Yep — I always knew I'd have a little girl — called Vivien.'

She looked puzzled. 'Vivien — why Vivien?'

He grinned. 'After Vivien Leigh — Scarlett O'Hara, of course.'

The penny dropped.

'Oh. Well, if it's a boy we shall call it Clark.'

Bill did a mock Southern drawl. 'Frankly my dear, that's fine by me.'

She gave a little chuckle.

He got up. Their eyes met.

He leant forward. Their kiss was long and poignant. Swallowing hard he straightened. 'I love you.' His voice was tight.

With that he was gone. It happened so

suddenly that for a while she thought he would come back into the room. When he didn't the awful realization that she was on her own made tears well up.

She got up, threw her napkin on to the table, and fled, just making their room before she burst into uncontrollable sobs. Mary lay down on the rumpled unmade bed and pressed her face into her pillow as she cried her heart out.

They assembled in the operations hut and clustered around a blackboard, sitting in chairs and on the ends of tables.

' 'Shun!' came from the doorway.

They snapped to attention as the Squadron CO and Group Officers marched in. When they were at the blackboard with its covering curtain the CO gestured to them to sit down. They sat or lounged at the back, all attentive. The CO would normally hand over for the Group briefing, but today he turned and faced them all.

'Gentlemen, as you well know the *Wehrmacht* has been giving our men a hell of a time in the Ardennes. Well, the weather is at last good in the area, so we are going to support the tactical boys in a monumental low-level effort to shalak the Krauts off the face of the earth. They've got a supply bottleneck at Houffalize.' He paused, looked around. 'Your briefing will now follow. Go get 'em.'

Unusually there was a ragged cheer as all the pent-up frustration of the last few weeks came out.

For five days they flew sortie after sortie, strafing roads behind the lines. When nothing else moved on the tarmac they sprayed the ditches where they knew the enemy were hiding under cover, waiting for dark when they could start to make their night-time moves.

Everywhere burnt-out tanks, vehicles and abandoned materiel littered the landscape. In the face of the awesome Allied air power the German advance faltered, and without fuel, finally broke. Hitler's throw to divide the Western Front had failed, and at irreplaceable cost.

On day six Bill heard someone call excitedly over the R/T. 'There's a column down there, on the edge of the forest — a whole lot of them.'

He swivelled around, searching down to the right. Sure enough there was a large field with vehicles, tanks, trucks, fuel-bowsers, hidden amongst the trees at the edge.

In the right position, Bill instinctively rolled over into a dive, calling on the others to follow.

As the nearest tank being refuelled by hand from drums on the back of a truck crept into range, he began firing off a long burst, watching his explosive hits 'walk' up to the truck which blew up in a massive ball of flame, engulfing the tank.

His fire carried on through into others as he bore down on them, only pulling back the stick and going into a shallow turning climb to the left just above the deck. He flashed through the billowing smoke as others began their attack. Soon the area was full of great columns of smoke.

Time and again he dropped a wing and went back for more. When they couldn't see anything else to hit they reassembled at 4,000 feet. The CO's voice broke the silence.

'Good work boys. We're going home.'

They stayed low, still searching for targets of opportunity. As they passed near the town of Bastogne they saw a lot of army activity, and rows and rows of canvas bags.

Suddenly it sank home what it was.

Like everybody else, Bill's eyes followed the grim scene until it passed from view.

There, laid out in neat multiple rows had

been hundreds of dead GIs.

There was no let-up. Apart from the tactical necessity of their work, there had been a wildly spreading rumour of a massacre of American prisoners, which now fired a lust for vengeance.

Day after day nothing moved without the shadow of a Mustang travelling up the road at 400 miles an hour, spraying death and destruction.

But there was also a longing for the old days, for the 'clean' aerial battles with a valiant Luftwaffe. Contact with the enemy in the air was now almost non-existent, and even on the continuing bomber missions they had heard that the enemy was rarely seen — though a new propellerless fighter was to be feared.

So it came as a shock for Bill to see the thin shape of a fighter far below as they entered the operational sector at 10,000 feet.

It was too much of a temptation. With a quick word to the CO and without waiting for a reply, he rolled into a steep dive.

Bill concentrated on the black pencil-slim cross, occasionally glancing behind to make sure that the planes following him were friendly.

He caught up fast, and it was then that he

realized that the 109 was throttling back, entering the circuit to land on an airfield he hadn't seen: it wasn't on their maps.

When he was 200 yards behind he fired his first burst, scoring hits all over it. He pressed the button again, and was still hitting him when he had to stamp on the rudder and throw the stick to the right to avoid ramming him.

He looked back and saw the 109 dive straight down into the deck and explode. He was at 1500 feet now. Ahead was the airfield, with two 109s already landed. Bill pushed the stick forward, just as the flak opened up. Bright balls of fire came sailing up, seeming to move slowly until close, then whizzing by. He got right down on the deck. Little black clouds of flak with exploding yellow flashes inside them burst above him.

Instinctively he ducked, automatically taking evasive action, weaving and dipping, stamping one rudder then the other, skidding and side-slipping so that the fireballs never had a fixed line to zero in on.

The first 109 turned off the strip, trying desperately for shelter.

Bill triggered the button, saw his shells slamming into it, bits flying in all directions. The plane lost control, started to wander across the grass as his shells found the second plane. It blew up. Bill flashed over-head, banking away to avoid the trees at the airfield boundary.

At that moment there was a 'crump' and his plane shuddered. Bill smelt explosive, and there was a numbness in his leg. He knew he'd been hit, he eased the stick back. His plane responded only sluggishly. Gradu-ally he gained height but there was no doubt in his mind that she was mortally wounded, and that he'd have to get out.

He managed to coax the plane to 6000 feet and some twenty miles back towards the Allied lines when the oil-pressure gauge suddenly shot into the red, and flames began to stream back over the port side. It could only be a matter of minutes before she blew up.

Hands shaking, Bill freed himself from his radio and oxygen lines, released the seat harness, pulled back the hood. Then he took a deep breath, rolled the Mustang, and fell out, head first, into a whirling maelstrom of freezing air.

Mary was in the library when they called. There were three of them — two American Air Force officers, and the college chaplain.

At the sight of them, so alien to the sur-roundings, and their sombre faces, the blood drained from her cheeks. Her legs quivered, lost all strength. She grabbed at the back of a chair, held on for support as the room began to go round.

The older officer removed his cap, followed by the younger one.

'Mrs Anderson?'

'Yes.' Her voice was weak.

The man moved nearer, as if to help support her.

'Would you like to sit down?'

She wanted him to say whatever it was he had come to say — to blurt it out: her fear was taking all the strength from her body. She meekly slumped into the chair that the other officer held.

'Is it Bill?'

She'd spoken in a whisper.

The adjutant nodded. 'I'm afraid he failed to return from operations today.'

'Is . . .' she could hardly breathe '. . . he *dead?*' she asked, but it was unreal. There was no way he could be *dead* — not Bill.

'He's been classed as MIA.'

Mary struggled with her woozy head, still feeling faint. The adjutant seemed to think he needed to explain. 'That means missing in action — nothing more.'

The chaplain crouched down beside her, a crisp white handkerchief appeared from nowhere. 'Take this, my dear.'

Mary took the cloth, held it over her mouth and nose, brought her head down as she nearly passed out. After a while the chaplain said: 'Let's take you home, my dear.'

She shook her head. 'I want to be *there,* near the base, as soon as any news comes in. I want to know — I *must* know.'

The adjutant patted her shoulder. 'Believe me, as soon as we know *anything* — we'll send, or call. I promise. But it could be days — weeks even.'

The other man nodded.

'I'll come myself, Mary — that's a promise.'

The chaplain said: 'Where's your coat, my dear? These gentlemen have very kindly said we can use their car to get you home.'

Reluctantly she allowed herself to be taken to the car. As they drove through the streets of Cambridge the words kept going round and round in her head.

*Dear God, please, please, may he be all right. . . .*

*Dear God, please, please, may he be all right. . . .*

There was a fuss with the landlady, who was worried about looking after her. The chaplain said the college would provide a small emolument for a week to cover her extra expenses. To Mary it was all inconsequential, like a living nightmare.

They made sure she was warm and lying on her bed, and then left. The landlady went off to make tea.

A hush descended.

A hush in which the seconds were counted off by the beats of her heart.

Seconds into minutes.

Minutes into hours.

If the news was bad she knew her heart would die.

Oh, she would live, because their baby — *his* baby — needed to be born, raised in love, told of his or her father.

Little Vivien, or little Clark.

But she would be dead *in* her heart.

There would be only the long, long wait until they were reunited once more. When the last enemy had been defeated.

He had floated down in the cold clear air, the earth between his swinging legs was snow covered, with great tracks of dark pine-woods. The sun was shining, the dazzling whiteness beneath his feet made it hard to judge height.

There was no sound other than the air passing through the rigging, until there was a shattering explosion behind him, booming and echoing from a long way off.

When he managed to turn round, pulling at his lines, he saw that there was a black column of smoke mushrooming up many miles away. It had to be his ship — this was confirmed when he saw squadron Mustangs circling and swooping over the area. Then he was in amongst trees and he suddenly smacked into a snowdrift. Mercifully the impact was softened by its depth.

There was no wind: the canopy settled over him like a gently collapsing tent.

Quickly he snapped the release buckle, pulled the webbing off, and crawled out to the edge of the silk, uncovering his head and taking his first ground view of the land about him.

Gingerly he got up and tried putting his weight on his numb leg. To his surprise it took it, but his trouser leg was heavily blood-stained.

Quickly he bundled the 'chute into the hole his body had made, and pushed more snow over to cover it. He had no idea where he was: whether he was in German-held territory, or Allied, so it seemed to be a good idea to hide for a while.

He limped deeper into the trees. The woods were not like the tranquil oak and beech woods of England, but more like the northern forests of the States and Canada. Fir and birch predominated, and the sandy soil was covered with pine-needles and thin layers of snow.

He stumbled on, becoming acutely aware of the numbness in his leg turning to soreness, and finally a throbbing pain. He slumped down, back against a tree-trunk and looked at the blood caked on the fabric of his pants.

Bill could see that his fur-lined flak-boot had protected his leg below the knee, and the bucket seat had shielded his body, but the back of the leg was peppered with little pieces of shrapnel. As he raked with his finger a larger piece came free on one side of the knee — it had gone right through the fleshy underpart and come out on the side. He was still wearing his Mae West inflatable life jacket. Bill took it off and found the escape kit in the pocket. Inside was a first aid section. Wincing with pain he doused the area with the iodine. He felt weird, lightheaded, and began to shiver, and knew that delayed shock was beginning to take over.

He wriggled deeper into some bushes, pulling the Mae West with him, and began covering himself with the pine needles and sandy soil, both for camouflage, and to try to keep warm.

Stuck in the top of one of his boots was an air map. Bill took it out, studied it, finding difficulty in focusing. Eventually he realized that he had only a rough idea of where he was — the airstrip wasn't on it — but the big question was, which side of the front line was he on?

Cold, hungry and frightened he found a bar of high-energy candy. With shaking hands Bill broke off a piece and rewrapped the rest, determined to conserve it as long as possible. In between chewing he paused, listening for the sound of dogs, or voices shouting commands in German. He was aware only of an intense silence. No bird sang as the darkness of night, made to seem darker by his condition, drew around him.

He thought of Mary. What was she doing? Bill realized that by now they might have sent someone to see her, to tell her that he would not be coming home that night.

And for all she knew, he might not be coming home — *ever.*

The agony stayed with him through a sleepless cold night.

Cold as the grave.

The early morning light slowly suffused the room. She'd not slept, just lain on her bed, staring out through the window-panes at the starlit sky. The night had been full of the sound of the RAF on its way to Germany, and now the dawn chorus of war rumbled once again in the brightening sky — the incessant reminder of the deadly struggle that had consumed all their lives.

And Bill was somewhere over there — she just *knew*. He'd sworn never to leave her — he would be back. Please God, make it true.

Every time the phone down in the hall had rung she'd tensed so badly that she feared for her unborn child. But it had never been for her — so far.

Slowly she got off the bed. Her whole body was aching. She moved to the window and looked down into the garden — now turned over to vegetable production and with rabbit- and chicken-runs.

Ice covered the corners of the panes, and the fields beyond were white, but there had been no more snow.

But it was still bitterly cold. She put her fevered brow against the freezing glass, and cried gently, the first tears of the day.

He was so cold that he seemed to have stopped shivering, and the pain in his hands had begun to recede. Bill realized he was in danger of getting frostbite. He crawled out and stood up stiffly, clutching his hands under his armpits.

In the distance, about 200 feet away, he could see a sunlit glade. He staggered and crashed through the undergrowth until he got into the open sunlight.

He was still swinging his arms and cursing when he heard something. He stood rock-still, then his cold, blue face, with eyebrows covered in hoar-frost suddenly, painfully, grinned. In the far distance guns rumbled again. The front line.

He started in the direction of the sound, moving as quickly as he could, conscious that another night like the last might finish him off. In the escape kit was a compass. Although the rumbling echoed confusingly all around, he got a rough bearing.

Soon he realized how weak he was, and the going got harder and harder. With his hands he scooped some virgin snow, got it into his mouth through cracked lips.

As the day wore on the sound of the artillery repeatedly came and went. About two hours after he'd started his trek he heard planes overhead. They too came and went; the silence returned; the guns had gone quiet.

He so desperately wanted to lie down, but the thought of the night kept him going.

At midday Bill suddenly knew he must be near a road. He could hear, and sometimes see, aircraft flying up and down, obviously searching for targets.

He took more care. Eventually the trees thinned and he could make out a strip of tarmac. Crouching from tree to tree he got nearer, sank down and waited. His breathing was ragged, his body racked with pain. Utter exhaustion slowly overtook him. Despite his best efforts, his eyes finally closed. . . .

Bill was with Mary who had a little baby in her arms, his baby, which she was rocking from side to side in the warm sunlight.

He was tickling it and making baby-talk, when the ground shook and an explosion engulfed them in an orange flame.

Bill came to as the ground shook again. Ice and snow rained down in a dense cloud from the trees. Disorientated and half blind he struggled up into the fog. Voices were shouting and screaming. It was seconds before he realized that they were German. Bill sank down again, behind the tree, trying to make sense of his surroundings. In the blueish gloom he suddenly realized that it had grown late, and that a German convoy had obviously risked pulling back — and had been caught in a strafing run. As if to confirm his conclusion the snarl of an aero-engine, whining in a dive, grew louder. It was another attack. He burrowed down in the earth and snow as other figures ran into the woods, doing the same. Bill was among the enemy.

The cannon-shells and rockets started ripping into the convoy. As the first plane flashed past he recognized it as a British Typhoon.

Explosions shook the earth he was clinging to, black acrid smoke drifted between the trees, machine-gunfire kept up a continuous background clatter. With deafening roars more low-flying Typhoons swept past at fifty feet, white stripes on their wings showing that they were from the Second Tactical Air Force.

It lasted less than a minute. When silence returned he cautiously raised his head. Black columns of smoke rose into the air from several points. His ears slowly perceived the sound of crackling flames, shouts and swearing.

Bill watched as German troops, their field-grey uniforms a shock to his senses, ran back to the column, and began pulling bodies from the wrecked vehicles.

An officer barked orders as he directed the work. Bill waited, terrified of discovery.

He knew that if he was found, they'd shoot him out of hand, or beat him to death with spades. Troops who'd just been strafed would have no pity on a downed flier.

With much shouting and crashing of boots the convoy was sorted out. In less than ten minutes those vehicles that were still useable were pulling out, troops riding on every available space, their faces pale, drawn, unshaven, the glazed eyes those of soldiers on the edge of extreme fatigue.

A defeated army in retreat.

Only the blackened, still-smoking carcasses of vehicles remained. And the dead.

Bill crawled in closer, waited, despite the overwhelming urge to search for food and warmth.

Eventually he got up to the remains of a half-track troop-carrier, its blackened hulk containing charred bodies, eyeless bony faces frozen in grinning horror. A smell of cooked human flesh filled the air. Bill thanked his bloody stars he was in the Air Force.

He stood near to the steel plating, which was still glowing with heat. He began to feel his frozen body grow warm and pain come into his limbs. He kept a constant look-out, but nothing moved except for a couple of crows searching through the carrion.

Later, he found some rations. He fought down the urge to stuff himself, found a knapsack and crammed in chunks of black bread and cheese, all the time looking around.

What to do next?

Bill looked at the woods, and then down the long straight road towards the front line — which had gone eerily quiet. He would have liked to carry on, but his body was incapable.

With the decision to stay, the realization came that he had to be warmer than he had been last night.

He went to the next wreck, a truck, aware of the rapidly failing light. The Germans would be coming out in droves soon: retreating.

Bill put a foot on the burnt out, tyreless wheel and hauled himself up. As his eyes reached the top a German soldier lunged at him. With a scream Bill fell, landed heavily on his back. Winded, he couldn't move.

But no figure appeared above to finish him off. No sound, no nothing.

When he got his breath back he crawled around to the other side, stood up, swaying, and then cautiously climbed up.

The dead soldier had fallen on to his face, and then rolled over on to his back, hands clasped to his belly, intestines spilling out. He was stone-dead, sightless eyes white in the gloom. When Bill got over the shock he began to search, finding a couple of half-burnt blankets, a sergeant's greatcoat, albeit flecked with blood, and a trenching tool.

He'd just got his little hoard into the wood when he heard the sound of another convoy. Hidden, he waited, watching the column drive past before he stirred.

Bill got the overcoat on over his flying jacket, spread one blanket into the depression he'd dug, got into it and brought the other one over him, putting sand and pine needles back over him as much as possible.

He was not unaware that it was like a shallow grave.

He ate some bread and cheese, took a swig of water and tucked down, head under the blanket, feeling pleased with himself. Bill went to sleep so quickly it was like passing out.

But only for a couple of hours. When he awoke with a start, he thought at first it was because of the awful cold coming up through the earth. He struggled upright, used both blankets to cover his shoulders and head, and huddled back against a tree. But then he realized there was something else. The ground shook again, like an earth tremor, and he saw that the sky to the north east was angry red, a shepherd's delight — except that it was man-made, with sudden beads of intense light expanding out with lightning speed in widening rings to the stars.

Seconds after each one the earth quivered, followed further seconds later by deep detonations.

The RAF was pasting something — using their fearsome Tall Boy bombs by the feel of it.

Behind and to his left the night sky was also rent with great flashes, flickering like sheet-lightning: the front line.

Eventually he was aware of smaller sounds — the steady roar of traffic on the road half a mile away, and, incongruously, an owl screeching like a madman in the wood.

Bill tried to get down under his blankets again, overcome with the feeling that the whole world was coming to a violent end.

*Götterdämmerung:* the twilight of the gods: of one god.

Hitler.

The madman in the woods screamed again. Bill could only guess at the unimaginable horror that was going on all around him.

Would he ever see Mary again in this life?

■ ■ ■ ■

Mary decided that she could take the waiting in her room no longer. She called the
squadron office yet again, was told there
was still no news, and then informed them
of what she proposed.

The adjutant came on, sounding concerned. 'My dear, is that wise? We can
contact you so easily where you are.'

Unseen she nodded. 'Yes, it's what I want.'

The adjutant relented. 'I'll send someone
down into the village straight away.'

When she rang off, the adjutant sat back,
chewing on a pencil. He liked the girl very
much, what he'd seen of her, but he wondered if she was really grasping the reality
of the situation. Other pilots in the squadron
had seen Bill's plane go barreling down and
explode. No sighting had been made of a
'chute.

That was several days ago now. It wasn't
looking hopeful. He'd already given orders
for Bill's effects to be boxed, ready to give
to her.

Now she wanted to come and live in the
village, to be nearer. It didn't sound healthy
to him. All the same he sent a trusted PFC,
on a bike down to the village to ask around,

starting at the local pub. He really didn't want her around the squadron: it wouldn't be good for moral.

He called her back later in the afternoon, saying quickly, without preamble, so that she wouldn't jump to the wrong conclusion and think it was news about Bill:

'We've found a room — on a farm, right beside the airfield. They'd be happy to have you — it's five shillings a week, and I gather that includes home-grown and cooked breakfast and dinner.'

The adjutant had had a change of heart, and arranged transport for her from the station. He wanted to do what he could for Mary, because arrangements for the transfer to mainland Europe had now been finalized.

By the time that took place, or earlier, they should be in a position to know for certain what Bill's fate had been.

The Germans were falling back steadily, although with occasional pockets of resistance, but the area where his ship had gone down should be in Allied hands in days, and the drawn-out agony for her would be over.

For Mary it was strange, the first sight of his base with its MPs manning the barrier, their helmets and webbing white, which was

246

why they were called 'Snowdrops' — said her driver.

This was home to Bill, where he had lived when she first met him.

After they passed the main gate she could see aircraft and huts in the distance. The adjutant had promised that he'd arrange for her to visit soon.

The car turned up a drive set in trees. After about half a mile they emerged in front of a half-timbered farmhouse adjacent to the airfield, its thatch roof sadly in need of repair. The jeep stopped in front of the oak door. As she got out, a flight of three Mustangs roared over the house, peeling off to land one by one in the far distance.

Seeing the planes coming home in the evening sky, like birds to roost, was immeasurably sad.

Bill should have been home, should have been with her. But until he was, she felt nearer to him here.

And he would feel her presence — fly home to *her.*

Bill had started to walk along the middle of the road. Sometimes he realized what he was doing, sometimes he was back home, walking to get gas for his car.

His leg ached and he knew he was hot, so

much so that he had undone his great coat.

He heard the column coming even before it appeared around the bend, but when he turned his relief broke through his fever.

It was an American convoy, led by several jeeps with MPs and brass — a colonel or something — in the second one.

He stood and waved with his arms until they ground to a halt.

'Am I glad to see you guys.'

Nobody moved for a second, then the colonel got out and, accompanied by two MPs, advanced towards him.

Bill, swaying, awaited their greeting — then realized he had on a German great coat.

'Hell.' He tore it off. 'I'm no *Kraut*.' He drew himself up. 'First Lieutenant William Anderson, sir, United States Army Air Force.'

The colonel did not react to his salute. Bill frowned, began to get an odd feeling. Then the colonel spoke, in excellent English.

'But unfortunately for you, I *am* a *Kraut*.'

It took a few seconds for it to sink in.

Shocked Bill suddenly realized it was one of the units that had penetrated behind American lines, causing havoc and outrage.

The officer's face hardened. 'So, you are a pilot?'

Bill nodded.

It was weird, hearing an American officer say: 'You have been strafing our troops?'

Through his delirium Bill suddenly realized that he was on a knife edge.

He lied.

'No, bombing a railway bridge.'

The colonel's white face, tired and drawn, was stony.

'So, you are a Terror-*flieger*. You are a murderer of innocent civilians, of women and children.'

At that moment Bill knew he faced imminent death. The officer snapped an order in German. The two MPs on either side of him roughly ripped open his shirt top. One produced a knife, and for a split second he thought they were going to cut his throat. All he could think of was that he had let Mary down.

Having survived the crash he was still going to die, murdered on the whim of a passing Nazi. Then he felt his dog tags pulled violently forward and the cords severed.

They were passed to the officer who glanced down at them, then tossed them away into the bushes. He flicked his head at the two MPs who stepped aside, and drew out his issue American Officers sidearm.

The 'Colonel' raised it, pointed it straight at his head. At less than five feet he couldn't miss. Irrationally Bill heard the whine of attacking aircraft.

He tensed up, but could only feel a great sadness: that he would not see Mary again or ever see his child; be there for school, for university perhaps, and his or her wedding.

Would there be grandchildren who would never know him?

There was a deafening explosion, and Bill Anderson's world ceased to exist.

# CHAPTER TWELVE

It was a month since Winston Churchill had announced to the nation that Germany had surrendered, unconditionally; since the cheering crowds had blocked Whitehall, the Mall and all the main roads in central London; since his appearance on the balcony of Buckingham Palace with the King and Queen and the Princesses Elizabeth and Margaret Rose.

Mary paused, checked the address of the large Whitehall building and went in through the imposing Portland stone entrance.

At the reception desk she was directed to the third floor. The corridor was wide, high-ceilinged, with a marble floor and a long Persian carpet. Busts of frowning men in classical robes lined its sides.

It had obviously been built at the height of Britain's Empire days, when Queen Victoria, Empress of India, was on the throne.

251

She found the door she wanted and went into a small ante-room. A pair of velvet-covered sofas stood against two walls. A man behind a small but exquisite desk stood up and came around to meet her, hand held out.

'Mrs Anderson?'

She took his hand as he continued:

'Sir Anthony is expecting you — this way.'

He went to large double doors, tapped and waited, ear near the wood. She heard a garbled: 'Come in.'

The man shot her a smile, said: 'Excuse me,' and led the way in, announcing 'Mrs Anderson, sir.'

As Sir Anthony rose with outstretched hand from behind a huge ornate desk, his secretary scurried to place a chair behind the woman who was so obviously with child.

Mary sat down.

'Thank you for seemg me, Sir Anthony.'

The man she addressed wore a dark pin-stripe suit, with old-fashioned lapels. A silk handkerchief was draped from his top pocket.

Although his face was lined with age and good living, his hair was still brushed back in a thick wavy mane.

'Not at all — not at all.'

He opened a leather-bound, frayed file

and shuffled through some papers.

'As you know, Sir George personally asked me to look into your request. He speaks very highly of your service to His Majesty's Government — your work at Bletchley, I gather?'

She gave a quick, humourless smile, but said nothing.

Sir Anthony cleared his throat.

'Now, about this matter of your husband, First Lieutenant Anderson of the American Army Air Force posted missing in action — presumed killed.'

It was as though someone had kicked her in her swollen belly. 'He's *not* dead. They have found what's left of his plane — but no trace of him. He must be injured — lost his memory — but not *dead*. I know it.'

The Whitehall mandarin recoiled under the unfamiliar display of emotion and, embarrassed, picked up one of the papers.

He coughed. 'Quite so. Well, we've reviewed the documents supplied by our American allies, and all the other services, Army, Navy, Air-Sea Rescue, and the Commission for Displaced and Missing Persons.'

He looked up at her.

'Of the thousands and thousands, we've narrowed it down to maybe a couple of hundred people, given that he had —'

quickly he changed to '*has* an American accent and concentrating on the area where he was reported missing. Oh, and of course, he doesn't know who he is and has no means of identification.'

He felt like saying that it was all rather ridiculous, but refrained. The woman was obviously emotionally unstable. He pushed across the list.

'Pardon me for saying so, but I thought he would have been wearing military identity discs, so I do not see how he could go unidentified?' Mary dismissed him as she continued to read the list of locations and the men held there who could not be identified.

'There must be some explanation.'

Sir Anthony looked at his hunter. It was time for lunch at his club.

'As you can see, many are in hospitals, both military and civilian, and in holding areas in France, Holland, and of course Germany. I've anticipated your need to travel in these areas and have prepared the necessary documents. The Americans and the RAF have kindly found room for you on some of their transports — you can fly like that, can you?'

He nodded in the general direction of her body.

Mary frowned. 'Yes, apparently.'

'It's going to be pretty strenuous you know. Are you sure it's wise?'

'Wise?' Mary folded the paper and picked up the file that he had pushed nearer. 'Wise doesn't come into it, Sir Anthony. It's something I've got to do.'

She stood up and held out her hand, which he took as she continued: 'I appreciate all you have done for me as I'm sure you are very busy. There is so much to do, isn't there?'

Sir Anthony buzzed the intercom.

'Think nothing of it. Sir George says that you were most helpful to the code-breaker people — some nuance of the language, I believe. Do you know, I had no idea you people existed — most still don't.'

Mary gave a weak smile, eager to be on her way. The secretary came in, and stood holding the door open.

Mary said: 'Thank you once again,' and left.

When she'd gone Sir Anthony mused to his secretary: 'A sad case that I fear will have no happy ending. The Americans have privately admitted that they believe he is dead. I know these are exceptional times, but really, I don't see the point of letting women take degrees — they remain as emotionally immature as ever.'

Mary flew from RAF Northolt to a cold, wrecked Berlin. The sight from her small window both amazed and deeply depressed her. Mile after mile of ruins. It was as if some enormous earthquake had devastated the place. What so-called civilized men did to each other was far worse than any savage could devise.

She stayed overnight in a transit hotel. Next day she began her search.

The first wooden camp was on the outskirts. After having her papers inspected at the gate, she was shown to the medical block. Mary spoke in fluent German to the doctors, who then took her to see a whole ward of decrepit, broken men, some clearly mentally disturbed, who just lay or stood around smoking.

The doctor explained: 'These are the ones who fit your profile. Some have a few words of English, but they do not speak it like a person from America, in my judgement. Others don't speak at all — are mute.'

Mary realized that an accent would be useless as a guide under these conditions. She walked among them, conscious of their staring eyes, some lustful, even in her condition, some hopeful — most just blank. There was an all pervading smell of disinfectant, urine, and necrosis.

Outside she began to cry, not knowing whether it was the daunting scale of the task she had set herself, or the sight of so much broken humanity.

For the next month the story was the same — visit after visit; pitiful souls with no past, no future.

With a sinking heart Mary, for the first time, faltered. Her condition was not helping — her ankles had begun to swell and an army doctor had said she had high blood pressure and needed bed-rest.

She gave herself seven more days and cheered herself up with the resolve to come back after she had given birth.

At the end of the week she was packing her brown case when the bedside telephone rang. When she answered, a man speaking in German, explained that he was a doctor at a local civilian hospital, and had heard from a colleague at a Red Cross camp which she had just visited.

Mary, phone cradled between shoulder and ear, carried on with her folding and packing.

'You know why, I assume?'

The voice in her ear said: 'Yes, of course Frau Doktor. We have two men here, with absolutely no identity. Both mute, with serious head injuries. One was found with the corpses of dead German soldiers who had been killed by aircraft cannon-fire. They were disguised as American soldiers. I don't know if that is significant.'

Mary looked at her watch. She had an hour before the jeep was due to take her to the American airbase twenty kilometres away.

'Very well. I'll come immediately. Thank you.'

She took the address, finished packing and delivered her case to the hotel clerk. 'Tell the driver to wait — I shall be very quick,' she instructed.

'Of course, Frau Doktor.'

She'd found long ago that the use of her academic title worked wonderfully in the strictly organized German society.

In the event the hospital was in walking distance. Despite her condition she made her way through the cobbled streets lined with linden trees. The town had missed the worse ravages of war. At the top of a small hill she rested for a moment on a low wall before the municipal hospital.

The doctor, who turned out to be a round little man with pebble-like glasses, met her and led the way down the corridor.

'This was the one found dressed as an

American.'

He pushed his way through double doors.

A man was sitting in a chair by the window, dressed in striped pyjamas. As they walked towards him he turned and looked at her.

Mary's spirits slumped. Despite all the disappointments of the last few weeks, she always felt the same crushing despair. The man was not Bill.

She thanked the doctor and started to leave.

'Mary?'

The voice was a croak, so low that she thought she had imagined it.

Still walking, she turned her head. By a locker in the corner was another man in similar striped pyjamas. Emaciated, gaunt, eyes sunken beneath a bandaged forehead, he was a bag of bones.

Mary faced Bill.

A very tiny tear formed in the corner of one of her eyes as the doctor stood beside her.

'Oh, this is the other one. He was found in a bombed-out children's hospital.'

Mary swayed, almost collapsed, but the baby gave her a terrific kick.

She swallowed. 'Your admission records are at fault here, Doctor.'

The light flashed off the pebble-glasses as the flustered man consulted his notes.

'How do you know? It was hell at the end, we were overwhelmed. He does not speak, either.'

Mary advanced to Bill, held her hand out, frightened to hug the bag of bones in case she hurt him.

'He just did.'

Their fingers met.

# THE PRESENT

Mary stirred first.

'Bill, it's time. Tell me now.'

So he did, ending with: 'So that's it. A year, the doc says — maybe more, probably less.'

Mary held out her arms. He leant over and they held on to each other. She stroked his hair, kissing the top of his head as she had when she had comforted the children: Clark, Vivien and Mary.

Softly she whispered: 'Remember that first week, after we found each other again?'

His voice was muffled.

'I know darling but —'

She shushed him. 'No buts. We swore then that we would never be parted again — *ever.*'

Mary released him and eased him up so that his face was opposite hers. She searched him with an intense, almost fevered eye.

'It's time.'

Frightened at the enormity of what she was proposing he tried to argue.

'Mary you could. . . .'

She was adamant.

'I meant it then and I mean it now.'

Bill swallowed. He knew that voice of old, the young and determined 'bluestocking'.

'When?'

Mary smiled. 'Tomorrow.'

Back in Cambridge he went along to the American Cemetery at Madingley, stood looking down at a couple of the simple white crosses among the rows and rows. He took longer finding names among the hundreds on the Wall of Remembrance — those who had no known resting-place. That evening they treated themselves to a superb dinner at a favourite watering-hole. Champagne flowed.

They clinked their glasses in a toast.

Mary proposed: 'To us.'

'To us,' he responded. 'And the last mission.'

They didn't sleep at all that night — but sat up talking, writing letters to the children, and just sitting before the fire looking through photograph albums — many of the photographs were in black and white. They consigned hundreds to the flames.

In the morning the fire was cold, dead. As

he looked around for the last time, Bill's gaze fell on the grey ashes. It was over.

They used the MG to go to the flying club, Bill roaring in and skidding to a halt on the gravel. Mary berated him.

'Stop showing off, you old fool.'

He got the wheelchair from the back and set it up. Mary, hanging on to the windscreen and the door, settled into it. She called to him as he went back round to the driver's side.

'Don't forget the CD player.'

Bill grumbled. 'What did your last slave die of?'

He wheeled her into a hangar. Light aircraft were parked inside, some, their engines exposed, were being worked on by mechanics. They made their way to a door in the side wall marked 'Office'. When they entered a man was at a chart marked 'Aircraft Availability', writing with a felt-tipped pen in the squares alongside the registration numbers.

He turned, saw the elderly couple, the woman in a wheelchair.

'Ah — is it Mr Anderson?'

Bill held out his hand. 'Sure is.'

They shook. Bill indicated Mary.

'And this is my wife.'

'How do you do. Now, I gather you want an hour's pleasure trip — is that right?'

Mary nodded. 'Yes — see some old haunts — where we met — seems like centuries ago.'

'Right. Well if you're ready . . . ?'

Bill grinned. 'All set and raring to go.'

The man selected some keys from an open wall-cupboard.

'Right.'

Outside they reached a sleek low-wing aircraft with a single piston engine.

Bill gave a whistle.

'Jeez, she looks fast.'

The man nodded proudly. 'Can do two hundred-plus knots.'

Bill ran a hand appreciatively on the wing. 'I used to fly with Pan Am, and before that in the war.'

Surprised, the pilot, opening the door, said: 'Did you, now? What were you on?'

Bill brought the wheelchair to the rear door. 'Ended up on 747s.'

The pilot's enthusiasm was obvious. 'And during the war?'

'Mustangs.'

'Really? That's terrific.' He slapped the fuselage. 'Not so exciting as a Mustang, I'm afraid, but she's lively enough.'

Bill nodded. 'Expensive to run, I bet. Fully

insured, of course?'

'Oh yes. Costs an arm and a leg.'

Light-heartedly Bill chuckled.

'Worth more to you wrecked, I guess.'

The man laughed.

'Yes — but the trick is making sure you walk away in one piece.'

Mary glanced at Bill as he said: 'You bet.'

They helped her into the rear, Bill saying: 'I'd like to be in the co-seat, if that's OK with you?'

'Sure. Can you get in yourself while I put Mrs Anderson's wheelchair in the office?'

'No problem.'

As he trotted off with the chair, Bill made his way around to the other door. He looked in at her, and nodded just the once.

'OK?'

She finished buckling her seat belt.

'OK.'

Bill ran his eye over the instrument panel as the pilot went through the take-off procedures and check list, then taxied to the strip.

When eventually he released the brakes the little aircraft positively shot down the runway and was in the air and climbing in no time.

Bill watched intently as the pilot raised

the undercarriage and trimmed up the aircraft. When he was done he checked the route with Bill. 'Cambridge area, the coast and back via your old airfield?'

When Bill agreed, the pilot informed the tower. Within minutes they were over Cambridge. Bill and Mary looked down at the colleges, with Kings College chapel clearly standing out by the Cam as the river slowly passed by. Eventually the city receded from view.

Bill nodded to the right. 'Over there. Can you pass by that church, please?'

'No problem.'

They banked gently away. They both saw the winding lane that ran from it and its scattering of old houses, until she pointed. 'There.'

Sixty years had passed, and although some trees and green spaces still remained, the village had largely been engulfed by a huge housing development.

But they still recognized the cottage — *their* cottage, now on the edge of a park.

They watched it intently until it was nearly lost from view.

Mary waved a final goodbye with just her fingers and turned back. Their eyes met. She lowered her lids, and mimed a soft kiss at him in memory of their first time to-gether.

The pilot banked again. 'We're on our way to the coast now — right?'

Bill agreed. They would have liked to have kept silent, lost in their memories, but the pilot was chatty.

'You been back before?'

Bill had to rouse himself from his thoughts. 'Actually I stayed over here after the war — based at Heathrow.'

He said nothing of the long years of devoted nursing by Mary, until he was fully back to normal. The doctors said it was a miracle. The bullet, instead of penetrating his skull, had travelled in an arc under his scalp, and exited at the back without ever damaging the brain directly. The force of the bullet, and the air pressure wave before it had, however, bruised the brain severely, leaving him with complete loss of memory. To that very day, nine months might never have existed as far as he was concerned. The pilot adjusted the throttle.

'Really? I would have thought there was more for you at home?'

Bill glanced back at Mary, grinned.

'Oh no, I had a lot going for me over here, what with being over-paid and over-sexed as well.'

He heard her cough.

The pilot chuckled. 'So, being here it's been easy for you to attend all the reunions, I suppose. Do you still go?'

Wistfully Bill shook his head.

'They finished a couple of years back. Not too many of us left — we're a dying breed.'

They lapsed at last into silence as Bill gazed down at the towns and villages of Suffolk and Essex that he knew so well from the skies of 1944: Sudbury, Braintree, Ipswich, Orfordness.

Just after they crossed the coast the pilot turned back, left the North Sea behind. 'Seen that many a time, eh?' he said to Bill.

Bill said sadly: 'Lost a few buddies down there.'

Using a wartime map he'd kept, Bill gave a course to the area of his old base. Suddenly the pilot pointed out of his side window and brought the plane around as he said: 'Over there. Doesn't look as if much of it is left. I'll go down.'

Bill took a deep breath.

'Say, no chance I could take her over it — just one last time?'

The pilot hesitated. The delightful old boy was certainly someone to be admired but, hell he must be eighty-odd years old.

He flicked a quick look at him. The man's

eyes were big and pleading.

'Well, given your experience — why not. You have control.'

Bill's face split into a huge grin as he placed his gnarled hands on the yoke.

'God bless you — I have control.'

'You have,' responded the pilot.

Bill flew her straight and level, getting the feel, then. . . .

'I'm going a little lower for a look-see — OK?'

The pilot grinned nervously.

'Sure.'

As they reapproached, Bill suddenly said: 'Here we go,' and pushed the stick forward, diving down and passing so low over the weed-covered airstrip and rusty control tower, that he had to pull up steeply to avoid a water-tower.

'Wowee.'

Shaken, the pilot reached forward.

'I'm taking control.'

Bill sang out. 'You have control.'

He grinned across the cabin.

'Sorry, don't know what came over me — just had to give the old base one last beat-up for old times' sake.'

The pilot looked pale, said nothing.

They landed back at the airfield, taxiing in and coming to a halt after the pilot had brought her round on the pan to face the field again. He cut the engine and silence descended. Almost immediately Mary groaned.

'I'm afraid my back is giving me terrible pain — could I get out quickly, please? I really feel awful.'

On cue, Bill unbuckled his seat belt, began to move — and winced.

'Hell, I've gone stiff — my new hip. Would you mind getting the wheelchair for my wife? She needs her medication urgently.'

The pilot cracked his door open, glad to get out.

'No problem.'

He jumped down, and walked away, deeming it necessary to break the training of a lifetime to get the old people off quickly — he'd complete post-flight checks in a moment. He left the keys in the ignition.

Bill found Mary's eyes. 'Well that's made it a damn sight easier.'

The pilot had just got the chair and was easing it out of the office door when he heard an aero engine start up. He didn't connect it with the aircraft he'd just piloted, but when he heard it taxiing almost immediately, he knew it had to be his, there had been no time for pre-flight procedures with a cold engine.

Leaving the chair he ran for the hangar door, in time to see his plane wallowing away across the grass making straight for the runway. He ran after it, actually reached the tailplane and held it for a moment, shouting into the roaring slipstream: 'Stop, stop, you old thief.'

His foot caught in a rabbit-hole, and he went face down into the mud. He could only watch as the plane reached the runway, turned into the wind and took off in text-book fashion.

From the back seat Mary said: 'I want to come forward, sit with you.'

He half-turned. 'Of course. I'm putting down in my old place. There's just enough runway left — I think.'

She rolled her eyes in disbelief.

When at last it finally came up on the horizon Bill said: 'Hang on gal — here we go.'

He bled off the speed, and lowered the undercarriage. Selecting the correct flaps as he had observed, Bill coaxed the machine down to just over the boundary fence, then killed the flying speed, dropping with a final thump right on the end of the old runway.

Mary yelled out in pain as he rammed hard on the brakes, the plane banging and juddering rhythmically over the uneven concrete sections. The smell of burnt rubber invaded the cabin.

They came to a halt with barely twenty feet of weed-covered runway to spare.

Bill sagged in the seat.

'Jeez, I'm getting too old for this.'

He brought the plane back to the other end, and turned again into the wind before turning off the engine. Mary had unbuckled by the time he opened her door and lowered the step. She clung to him as he eased her down.

Mary said: 'Hang on, I need to rest for a second.'

He set her down in the long grass and they lay side by side listening to the skylarks in the soft breeze.

Mary stared up into the heavens, her hair splayed out on the grass. Bill looked across at her, at this woman who had become part of him, and he part of her all those years ago: a lifetime.

He loved her even more now.

She suddenly sighed. 'It's just like the Inkspots said.'

Puzzled, Bill asked: 'What are you talking about?'

She smiled at him, put her hand over his, loved him lying there with a long stalk of

272

grass sticking out of the corner of his mouth, looking so boyish — just as he had when she had first set eyes on him and knew he was the one for her.

'The long grass — it's whispering to us.'

Bill lay in silence, chewing his stalk.

'What's it saying?'

Her face quickened with concentration. 'Let's see — How does that old poem go?

The sleep that I have and the rest that I
    have
— though death will be but a pause
For the youth of my life in the long green
    grass,
is yours and yours and yours.'

She rolled over on to him, put her hand gently on his cheek.

'It's not like the England of old is it, the decent innocent gentle place we all struggled for? Now it's so different: ill-mannered, drugs, violence — all of it. We don't belong any more in this age where sex is more important than love.'

He took the stalk from his mouth.

'Every generation says that, darling — it's just we've been lucky enough to grow very old and are able to look back through rose-coloured spectacles to our youth.'

She shook her head.

'I'm aware of that and know there are a lot of good people out there, but I truly believe the world is not so nice as it was. We've all gained materially but we've lost something — our *spirit* — in the process.' She paused, then touched his lips with hers, this man who had been her only lover — the only one she had ever wanted. 'Do you remember that night in the garden of the cottage — back in forty-four?'

He nodded. 'Of course.'

She whispered softly: 'Stars by the millions — big and bright. You don't see them much now, do you, with all the light we flood the heavens with? Well, who knows, where we are going, maybe the stars really will be beneath our feet. No . . .' Her warm voice that he knew so well was suddenly the old forties, cut-glass English of their first meeting in the library: the no-nonsense bluestocking.

'We don't belong in this world any more, darling. Let's find out what awaits us in the next — together.'

She gave a mock salute.

'*Our* last mission.'

Mary was free of pain — having swallowed a day's worth of tablets with the gin-and-tonics she brought ready-mixed for them both. Bill had doubled the strength of his dose, remarking at the label: 'Hmm, I'm not to drive a car it seems.' He grinned and pushed his chin into his chest — just like Cary Grant. 'It says nothing about flying a plane.'

With her strapped beside him, he faced the controls. 'Right, let's see if we can get this old bird off the ground again.'

She smacked his leg.

'Don't you talk about me like that. Have you got the CD player?'

He brought it up from the floor and gave it to her.

'All set?'

She nodded.

The engine burst into life. Bill checked his Ts and Ps. Everything was functioning as it should. 'The old strip's not what it was, so hang on to your hat.'

He gunned the engine, holding the little plane hard on its brakes. It trembled at the bit like a horse before a race, then he yelled:

'Brakes off, here we go into the wild blue yonder — like the old days.'

The plane leapt forward, slamming both their heads back against the rests. The runway passed under them faster and faster as a warehouse loomed larger, finally seemed to fill their whole world. Bill pulled back the stick, Mary's eyes widened; both gave an involuntary yell. . . .

They skimmed over the roof of the building, where men taking a smoke flung themselves flat on the deck.

Neither of them saw the police cars with flashing blue lights, which had been alerted by the pilot. He had guessed where Bill might have headed. The drivers got out of their cars, talking on their radios as the plane circled above them.

Bill looked down at the strip, gave a final salute, and headed for the coast as Mary turned on the CD.

To the tune of *American Patrol* they left the airfield.

On the ground, silence came again, except for the returned skylarks — and the whispering grass.

They flew around great cloud-castles, swooping and soaring, the sea sparkling below like molten silver where it was caught by the falling shafts of sunlight.

The music changed. With *Moonlight Serenade* he cut back the engine. The roaring gale outside slowly subsided.

Mary looked across at him. Their hands found each other, clasped tightly. Bill swal-

276

lowed, and mouthed silently: 'I love you.'

When the nose dropped Mary squeezed his hand even harder.

'Hold me.'

Bill pushed the stick forward and rammed the throttle through the gate.

Mary reached out, and Bill threw his arms around her. Faces pressed hard together, tears streaming down their cheeks, they held on tightly.

The plane passed into a cloud, engine screaming as the dive increased. When it came out into the open the glittering sea was rushing up at them.

Neither of them saw it.

Only each other.

# EPILOGUE

The little group stood in a fine rain. Moisture hung in the warm air like a mist. Among them were Mr and Mrs Clark Anderson, Vivien Hayes, neé Anderson and her husband, and Dr Mary Jean Anderson-Smith.

Earlier, in the little Church of Saint Gregory the Great, where their mother and father had gone in the midst of a terrible war, they had held a small memorial service.

Clark had spoken of his parents, and how they had met, and his father's recollections of the very peculiar war his generation of young flyers had fought — every bit as dangerous, every bit as lethal, every bit as nasty as any war that had gone before. Over 200,000 aircrew of all nations had fought and died in the skies over Europe.

Yet each time, immediately a mission was over, they went back to nearly normal living — as normal as it could be in wartime, with food, relatively warm and dry rooms, girls, tea in Cambridge, shows in London — and pubs.

There never had been a war like that in the history of the world. Probably never would be again.

Then, in accordance with the wishes expressed in the letters that had been sent to each of them and to the family solicitor, which had carried instructions on compensation if the aeroplane owner incurred any costs above the insurance pay-out, they had gathered outside.

Clark read a poem, its author unknown, and reached the last lines — modified by his father and mother.

Do not stand by our grave and cry
We are not there
We did not die

In the silence that followed a very strange thing occurred. The sound of a single piston-engined aircraft came from the west, grew in loudness, the noise eventually reverberating directly above them.

One of the little group, an eighty-four-year-old veteran of the Eighth Air Force knew a P51 Merlin-Packard engine when he heard it.

They all looked up, searching the lowering clouds.

But there was no sign of the aircraft. The engine noise receded, droned away into the east, towards a free Europe, and finally died.

Some physicists have postulated that there is an infinite number of parallel universes as the only way of explaining certain problems in cosmology. Therefore, it is entirely possible that even now a fresh-faced young woman with dark wavy hair, clasping several books to her bosom, is about to enter the library of her university. Inside, a young man in the uniform of an American pilot. . . .

Mary's spiritual interludes continue.

# ABOUT THE AUTHOR

**David Wiltshire** qualified as a dental surgeon from University College Hospital, London. He served his National Service as a dental officer in Aden and Singapore before returning to England. He is married with three children and six grandchildren and lives in Bedford. His novel *Nightmare Man* was adapted by the BBC as a four-part series.

We hope you have enjoyed this Large Print book. Other Thorndike, Wheeler, and Chivers Press Large Print books are available at your library or directly from the publishers.

For information about current and upcoming titles, please call or write, without obligation, to:

Publisher
Thorndike Press
295 Kennedy Memorial Drive
Waterville, ME 04901
Tel. (800) 223-1244

or visit our Web site at:

www.gale.com/thorndike
www.gale.com/wheeler

OR

Chivers Large Print
published by BBC Audiobooks Ltd
St James House, The Square
Lower Bristol Road
Bath BA2 3SB
England
Tel. +44(0) 800 136919
email: bbcaudiobooks@bbc.co.uk
www.bbcaudiobooks.co.uk

All our Large Print titles are designed for easy reading, and all our books are made to last.